Sherlock Holmes and the Lady in Black

JUNE THOMSON

Allison & Busby Limited
12 Fitzroy Mews
London W1T 6DW
allisonandbusby.com

First published in Great Britain by Allison & Busby in 2015.
This paperback edition published by Allison & Busby in 2016.

*All characters and events in this publication,
other than those clearly in the public domain,
are fictitious and any resemblance to actual persons,
living or dead, is purely coincidental.*

A CIP catalogue record for this book is available from
the British Library.

10 9 8 7 6 5 4 3 2 1

ISBN 978-0-7490-1997-6

Typeset in 11.5/16.5 pt Sabon
by Allison & Busby Ltd.

The paper used for this Allison & Busby publication
has been produced from trees that have been legally sourced
from well-managed and credibly certified forests.

Printed and bound by
CPI Group (UK) Ltd, Croydon, CR0 4YY

To Natasha and Susana,
with love and gratitude

CHAPTER ONE

Those of you who are familiar with the events that occurred during the latter part of Sherlock Holmes' life, after he had left our old lodgings at 221B Baker Street, will know that after giving up his career as a private consulting agent, he moved to Sussex where he took up beekeeping as a part-time livelihood.

His smallholding, or farm as he preferred to call it, was situated at Fulworth Cove on the South Downs, overlooking the sea and close to the village of Fulworth.

At this point I should warn readers that they would be wasting their time if they try to locate the places I have mentioned. Knowing Holmes' dislike of publicity, I have deliberately withheld their real names, a precaution that also applies to the people who are introduced in this account. So, for example, Harold Stackhurst really exists and was one of my old friend's Sussex acquaintances but you will not find him listed in any directory or index. Unlike my earlier accounts of his investigations, I have refrained from using footnotes unless essential for, while they are useful, they can at times be like obstacles in an otherwise smooth narrative path.

So to begin.

The following investigation took place in the summer of 1908. By that date, Holmes had already left Baker Street and had settled down on his little Sussex farm while I remained in London still working as a family doctor from my practice in Queen Anne Street. I had in the meantime remarried, an act that had caused a rift between Holmes and myself, who regarded my decision as a betrayal. I was hurt by his reaction although, considering his attitude to women and what he referred to sardonically as 'the softer emotions', it was not totally unexpected. This is one of the reasons why I rarely refer to my wife in my accounts, an omission that has caused some bewilderment, as well as curiosity among the Sherlockian commentators and my readers who have cudgelled their brains to discover her identity. I advise them that I am not about to divulge it for several reasons: first, because I consider my private life to be no one's business but my own and second, and perhaps more importantly, because I do not wish to rouse old resentments in Holmes himself. Suffice to say that I met her in 1901 during one of Holmes' inquiries and that we married the following year, in consequence of which I moved out of the Baker Street lodgings and bought my practice in Queen Anne Street, where I resumed my medical career.

My second marriage led to a complete breakdown in my relationship with Holmes that lasted for six months and although we were eventually reconciled, I was, however, only partly forgiven. Knowing he was too proud to make the first move, my wife recommended I bought two tickets for the production of 'Siegfried' at Covent Garden and posted one of them to him with a short note suggesting we met at the theatre and afterwards went to Marcini's, the Italian restaurant where we had dined after the successful conclusion of the Hound of the Baskervilles case.

He wrote back thanking me for the tickets and agreeing to meet me as I had proposed; so began a renewal of our former relationship, by no means as intimate as it had been when we had shared lodgings at 221B Baker Street but, as my wife pointed out, it might lead to a closer reconciliation.

It was an inspired suggestion on her part, typical of her generous, warm-hearted nature, and one that brought about the first signs of restoration in my relationship with Holmes, a man whom I am not ashamed to admit I revere.

From then on, we met in London, not frequently but every six months and gradually I began to feel some of that old intimacy returning little by little.

He never telephoned; he regarded that means of communication as an intrusion on his privacy although in his letters he did confide in me a few details of his new life in Sussex: for example, the acquaintances he had made such as Harold Stackhurst, the proprietor of a private school called The Gables; as well as aspects of his day-to-day life in Fulworth in which he evidently found great pleasure: long walks over the Downs, for instance, and the little lagoons left in the beach when the tide went out in which he would swim every morning; or the charm of Lewes, the nearest town, with its narrow streets lined with old houses.

On one occasion, he also referred to an extraordinary investigation that had all the overtones of his old Baker Street days of crime and detection. It concerned the death of Fitzroy McPherson, the science master at The Gables, and how another member of his staff, Ian Murdoch, the mathematics tutor, was for a time suspected of his murder until Holmes was able to prove his innocence.

Holmes himself had written an account of the case, entitled 'The Adventure of the Lion's Mane', which he said he would let me read one day, although he always failed to bring it when we met in London.

During this time, he never invited me to visit him in his Sussex retreat, an omission I could understand. He was leading a new life and, strong though our friendship had been, similar to his dislike of the telephone, he did not want his former life to intrude on his current one. I appreciated his reluctance to combine the two without resentment, grateful that we would go on seeing one another in London, a neutral meeting ground that held few intimate memories for either of us.

Therefore his letter inviting me to visit him in Fulworth for a week's holiday was a complete surprise that caused a certain amount of hesitation on my part. Of course I would accept; nothing would have stopped me from doing so, but at the same time a question mark hung over the invitation that made me feel a little unsure. Holmes never acted on impulse or out of any emotion, such as nostalgia or regret. There was always some rational motive behind his actions, including this one, I assumed, and I read through his letter several times hoping to discover some clue to the purpose behind his unexpected proposal. But I could find nothing. The letter was mainly concerned with directions as to how to reach his house by road, suggesting he assumed I would come by car. But why? Was it to save me the trouble of crossing London by train? I had no idea.

He wrote:

After you have reached Lewes, take the minor road signposted to Fulworth. Follow this for about three miles until you can see the tower of the local church, St Botolph's, on the horizon to the left. Shortly after it comes into view, you will see a narrow turning also to the left, Church Lane, which leads to my house, Bay Cottage.

I shall place a sign in the hedge directing you to it. I shall expect you to arrive at about 4 p.m. on Wednesday. By the way, bring a pair of rubber-soled shoes with you.

The letter concluded with the usual non-committal initials, *S. H.*

I was not at all disconcerted by the peremptory tone of his letter, remembering the message I had once received from him at the beginning of the Creeping Man inquiry, summoning me away from my medical practice: *Come at once if convenient – if inconvenient come all the same* – when apparently all he wanted to discuss with me was a monograph he proposed writing on the use of dogs in detection. It was then that I realised that, despite his occasional exasperation at the slowness of my mental faculties compared to his own brilliant intellect, he needed me as a kind of whetstone for his mind, in order to hone his own keen-witted talents.

So aware of the humble role I played in our friendship, I bustled about making the necessary arrangements for this unexpected visit: finding a locum to take over my practice in my absence; consulting maps for the journey; packing a portmanteau and, of course, writing to Holmes accepting the invitation; as well as buying a pair of rubber-soled shoes as Holmes had directed but for what purpose I had yet to discover.

It goes without saying that my dear wife, knowing how much Holmes' friendship meant to me and having suggested I contact him in the first place, raised no objection to my trip to Sussex, wishing me a happy outcome to my week's holiday. I could only hope that Holmes might meet her one day. His low opinion of women might be changed as a result but I knew there was scant chance of this happening.

Although I had reservations at first about driving so far, I found the journey, particularly the last stretch after Lewes, most enjoyable. I had bought a car, a modest Austin, mainly to make the home visits to my patients much easier and, to my own surprise, I had taken to this new form of transport with enthusiasm. It gave me a sense of freedom, even though I rarely drove far beyond the limits of my medical practice. The convenience, too, was very rewarding. There was no need to summon a cab and when it was cold or wet I could drive myself to any address without suffering from the inclement weather. In fact, it proved a benefit to my general health. The pain in my leg, the consequence of a wound I had received during my service as an army surgeon at the Battle of Maiwand in 1880 in the second Afghan war and which was particularly disabling during the winter months, almost disappeared. It was a great relief.

In fact, the only drawback to my drive to Sussex was the twisty nature of the road after I left Lewes. There were so many bends and corners, which I had to negotiate with such care, that I had few opportunities to observe the countryside I was passing through, apart from occasional glimpses now and then of splendid views of the sea to my right that lay sparkling in the sunshine like a shifting carpet of silver and, to my left, the gentle green contours of the Downs rising towards the horizon.

It was on this view that I tried to concentrate: looking out for the church tower that Holmes had stated was a landmark to the lane leading to his house. It was not easy to carry out any observation. There was a high, overgrown hedge to my left that obscured my view for much of the time and it was only when a gap appeared in the foliage that I could catch a glimpse of the church and at the same time keep a look out for the turning that led to the lane and eventually to Bay Cottage.

Then suddenly there was the church tower on the horizon and, with very little warning, there was a gap in the hedge beside which, propped up among the leaves, was a board with a broad white arrow painted on it pointing to the left, followed by an exclamation mark.

It was almost as much as I could do to brake, shift gears, indicate I was changing direction and at the same time turn the steering wheel to guide the car into the narrow opening.

My reaction to the situation was confused. On the one hand, I was delighted not to have overshot the turning; at the same time, I was somewhat exasperated by Holmes' lack of consideration. He had never learnt to drive and did not wish to do so. Like the telephone, he had little use for cars, considering them to be an intrusion on the peace of the countryside, and consequently he had no understanding of the techniques needed in driving, particularly on a winding road when one needed plenty of warning of where and when to turn.

The sound of twigs and small branches scraping along the side of the car also added to my impatience as I wondered what damage they were doing to the paintwork. At the same time, I was amused by the exclamation mark. It was typical of Holmes' cavalier attitude, on occasions, to the unwritten rules that governed the lives of most people, infuriating but in its way endearing in its eccentricity.

And suddenly he was there, standing in an opening in the hedge to my left and vigorously signalling for me to turn towards him; a familiar figure but at the same time so altered in appearance that for a second he seemed like a stranger. His skin was tanned by the sun and wind that, together with his hawk-nosed profile, made him look more than ever like a Red Indian chief.

He backed out of the gateway, beckoning me into a gravelled area where, getting out of the car, I stepped forward to greet him more formally. It was over five months since I had seen him and there was an air of restraint about our meeting as if neither of us was quite sure how to proceed. In the end, we simply shook hands, although Holmes showed an unexpected gesture of warmth and spontaneity by placing his left hand on my shoulder as if wanting to establish a more physical contact between us.

'Watson!' he exclaimed. 'My old friend! How good to see you!'

'And you too, Holmes,' I replied a little awkwardly, still not sure how to bridge the gap that inevitably had developed between us during the months we had been apart.

'Everything is all right, I trust?' he continued, leaning into the car to retrieve my portmanteau from the back seat.

His face was hidden from me so I could not see his expression but the careful neutrality in the tone of his voice told me he was referring to my second marriage which, as I have explained, had largely been the cause of the rift between us. Holmes is a man who does not need intimate relationships with other people, especially women. He prefers his own company and, apart from his brother Mycroft and myself, has no close friends. On the other hand, I like people, women included, and the death of my first wife, Mary Morstan, to whom I had been happily married for several years, had left an aching void in my life. But I can understand Holmes' feelings of betrayal.

And so, after several months of separation, we came to a compromise without a word being spoken. We would continue our old friendship but neither of us would mention my second wife, and from time to time we would meet. Of course, it was not the same as our former relationship and there were occasions when I mourned the loss of our old intimacy, when we had sat together before the fire in our Baker Street lodgings or the times when we had set off on one of Holmes' investigations and I had the privilege of seeing that great intellect of his at work.

I realised that this aspect of our relationship was over. Holmes had now retired. Even so, I had the feeling at the back of my mind that there was something more to this invitation to join him in Sussex for a week's holiday than a meeting of old friends. However, I could not puzzle out what it might be.

'Come in! Come in!' he was urging me, as he straightened up, my portmanteau in his hand. 'Let me introduce you to the little farm of my dreams!' he continued, throwing out an arm as if he were indeed inviting me to meet an actual person of whom he was very fond.

I was touched by the note of genuine affection in his voice, which I could understand as soon as I looked about me. It was a charming cottage built of whitewashed stone with small casement windows and a porch made of trellis, also painted white. Two more windows were set in the slope of the roof, both flung open, their glass panes catching the sunlight and, like mirrors, reflecting views of the garden that lay behind me. There were apple trees, I deduced, from the yellow and green fruit hanging on them like baubles on a Christmas tree. And under each one of them were small constructions, like a row of miniature cottages each with a peaked roof and white-painted walls, very similar to Holmes' cottage except they had no doors or windows. It took me a moment to realise that they were beehives, material evidence of Holmes' new way of life.

While I was puzzling this out, Holmes was striding ahead of me towards the front door of his own cottage and, flinging it open, stood to one side to allow me to pass inside.

I entered a large room that reminded me nostalgically of our former sitting room in Baker Street. There was a similar fireplace with a coal scuttle standing on the hearth, very like the one in which Holmes used to keep his cigars. There were also bookcases in the chimney alcoves, which I was certain contained the same volumes he would have brought with him from London: a copy of the current Bradshaw listing the railway timetables, an *Almanac de Gotha*, the catalogue of genealogies of all the European royal families, together with his own personally compiled commonplace books and encyclopaedias in which he pasted newspaper cuttings of any facts that he considered useful. The furniture was familiar also, being similar to Mrs Hudson's, our Baker Street landlady; a cane chair with cushions; a small, gateleg dining table together with four chairs and a sideboard complete with a tantalus holding two decanters of spirits, and a gasogene for making aerated water.

Everything was very neat and tidy and I was deeply moved, as well as astonished by the nostalgia that Holmes' choice of household goods suggested.

There were changes, of course. There were no heavy curtains at the window, which was flung open and the scene beyond was not at all like Baker Street with its houses and street lamps and brick walls. Here there were trees and bushes, their leaves glancing in the sunlight as the breeze stirred their branches, bringing with it the unfamiliar scent of the sea and warm earth.

My bedroom exhaled the same air of freshness and country odours. It was a small room simply furnished with a bed, a chest of drawers with white china handles, a cupboard in which to hang clothes and a washstand equipped with a jug and basin. Later I was to discover that Holmes' bedroom, next door to mine, was a mirror image and, although I looked closely about me, there was no sign of any of the paraphernalia associated with his old habit of injecting himself with a six per cent solution of cocaine.

Their absence delighted me. When we had shared the Baker Street lodgings, I had tried to wean him off the drug with only partial success. The evidence that the Sussex setting and the little home of his dreams had succeeded where I had failed gave me, I must admit, a small twinge of jealousy. I would have preferred to think that it was our friendship that had won him over at last. It was an absurd reaction and one that quickly passed, thank goodness. What really mattered was Holmes' health and well-being.

Two other rooms overlooked the back garden and the grassy incline of the Downs curving up towards the horizon with a distant view of the church. One was apparently his housekeeper's room, which was locked. From his letters to me I understood her name was Mrs Bagwell and that, although she was a good cook, she was too garrulous for his liking and that he had arranged for her to move in with her sister in the village during my stay, coming in on a daily basis.

The last room was also familiar. Here were the bottles and jars of chemicals, the test tubes and Petri dishes, the microscope and magnifying glass that had littered his scarred workbench in Baker Street – except that these articles were now neatly arranged and labelled. Other equipment stood about which suggested his new hobby of photography, which he had mentioned in one of his letters and that he apparently took very seriously. A black curtain at the window could be drawn to shut out the light when he was developing his photographs, samples of which were pinned to a cork display board on the wall or were pegged onto a cord that was stretched across the room like a washing line.

Holmes gave me only a few moments to look inside this room and I guessed from his haste that it was his holy of holies in which one was not supposed to linger. It was an example of his old tendency to secretiveness, however close his friendship might be to the observer.

Despite the haste with which he closed the door, I had the chance to look briefly about me and noticed that the developed pictures hanging up to dry were mostly views of the countryside and the sea, keenly observed and very professional looking. Among them were a few photographs of people, clearly not Holmes' first choice of subject matter apart from one individual whose likeness stood out from among the others. It was of a young woman in her early twenties, I surmised, and whose hair, despite the lack of colour in the black and white prints, I could envisage from the subtle tones of the photographs, as being a rich dark brown with auburn tints. As for her features, they were delicately moulded, particularly the mouth and the forehead. Her eyes were the same dark tone as her hair and looked out of the likeness with a gentle candour. The whole face had a clear, natural beauty and, although it may seem strange, I felt I could read into the photograph Holmes' tenderness towards the sitter, whoever she might be.

I later found out that her name was Maud Bellamy.

In all my years of friendship with Holmes, I have known him to be attracted to only one woman, 'the woman', as I once described her. She was, of course,

Irene Adler, the American opera singer who became involved romantically with the King of Bohemia. She was beautiful, intelligent and talented but there was a ruthless side to her character and although I thought she was the type of woman he might have married, any such romantic daydreaming on my part was soon shattered when she chose Godfrey Norton, a London lawyer, as her husband. Holmes, who was inadvertently called on to act as a witness at their wedding, kept the sovereign he was paid for his services and wore it on his watch chain as a memento, the only sentimental action I had known him make. Afterwards, he admitted that he had been outwitted by only one woman, presumably her.

In contrast, his relationship with Maud Bellamy seemed to be paternal.

Later, he stated that she would always remain in his memory as the most remarkable woman he had ever met and spoke admiringly of her perfect clear-cut features and the soft freshness of her delicate colouring.

At the time of my visit to Sussex I had not met her and, apart from the photograph, was unaware of her existence, so I put her to the back of my mind along with the feeling that there was more to Holmes' invitation than first appeared.

I slept well that night, tired from the long drive to Sussex and lulled by the sound of the sea, so different to the noise of London, a constant dull roar like that of some huge, restless creature prowling the streets of the city.

By the time I awoke Holmes was already up and, in the absence of his housekeeper, was preparing what he called a bachelor's breakfast consisting of coffee, toast and honey, of course, that he urged me to finish quickly so that we could escape from the house before the arrival of Mrs Bagwell.

'She will be here at any moment,' he explained, 'and if we don't leave soon, we shall be trapped here for half the morning. She knows you are coming and is eager to meet you. She has a stiffness in her neck, you see, and as I foolishly told her that you are a doctor, she is hoping for a free consultation. She means well,' he added as a more kindly afterthought.

'But . . .' I added with a smile.

'Exactly, Watson,' he agreed. 'Is there not a saying about the road to hell being paved with good intentions? Anyway, I suggest we take the rest of the day off while I show you the delights of Fulworth, the beach, for instance, and the cliffs. We could lunch at the Fisherman's Arms, the local inn. And, on the subject of food, that reminds me: Harold Stackhurst has invited us this evening for a meal at The Gables. I think you will like him, I find him very good company. So what do you say to my plan? A walk along the cliffs? A visit to St Botolph's? As my guest, you must choose.'

'I think a walk on the cliffs,' I replied. 'Like Mrs Bagwell, I am a little stiff from the drive from London, and the exercise will do me good.'

'Excellent!' Holmes exclaimed, giving me a sideways glance that was full of good humour and appreciation and I felt for the first time since my arrival that the gap between us was beginning to close.

CHAPTER TWO

The clifftop walk was most invigorating. The air was fresh and scented with the clean odour of salt and a more delicate aroma: wild thyme, I learnt later from Holmes. It was on this herb that the bees were nourished, the fragrance of which sweetened their honey and gave it its particular flavour.

After London with its streets and houses, offering little more to the eye than walls and chimneys, the view was magnificent, so wide and open that for the first few minutes of experiencing that huge sky and the broad, green sweep of the Downs, I felt overwhelmed by the sheer vastness of it all.

I began, too, with Holmes' help to pick out certain details of the landscape, for example, the inn he had mentioned, tucked away in the folds of the hills; the ancient stone walls of St Botolph's church; and, in the further distance, a more modern-looking building of red-brick with gabled roofs, aptly called The Gables, the previously mentioned residence of Harold Stackhurst, the proprietor of the private coaching establishment who had invited us to supper that evening.

Having admired the view, Holmes suggested we went down to the beach to take a closer look at the sea. It was a steep descent, made easier by a set of wooden steps and a handrail, constructed, I gathered from Holmes, after the Lion's Mane tragedy when the only means of reaching the cove was by a path so precipitous and slippery that it was dangerous to use. Some of the local inhabitants, including The Gables' staff who used the rock pools for swimming, Holmes himself and the proprietor of the Fisherman's Arms had clubbed together to pay for the steps and rail to be installed.

There was, I noticed, another set of steps on the far side of the bay and when I remarked on this, wondering why a second means of access was needed, Holmes explained it was private property, not available to the general public.

'That is rather ungenerous,' I remarked. 'Are they the owners of the house over there?'

I indicated a building at the top of the second

set of steps, partly hidden by trees and bushes that grew in the clifftop garden. Because of the foliage, it was difficult to make out much detail of the house except it seemed to be of the Regency period – for I glimpsed a pillared porch through the leaves and an upper tier of elegant windows, typical of that style of architecture.

As I spoke, I was aware of a subtle change in the atmosphere, as if a curtain had come down between us.

'Oh that!' Holmes replied in an offhand tone. 'That is Fulworth Hall. Now what do you think of the cove, Watson? It was worthwhile coming here, don't you agree?'

'Indeed I do!' I responded, for it was a magnificent setting.

The cove itself was a large semicircular bay surrounded on the landward side by steep rocky cliffs, the sea enclosing it on the far side. The beach immediately below the cliffs was composed of large pebbles like cobblestones, their surfaces buffed and rounded by the action of the waves over aeons of time. Further down, nearer the sea's edge, these stones were replaced by a wide swathe of sand with rocks strewn here and there, jutting out from the softer surface to form rough-sided pools, the largest of which contained seawater left behind by the receding tide. I remembered Holmes referring to the lagoons, as he called them, in one of his letters. It was in these that he usually bathed and I assumed the students and staff from The Gables made use of them for the same purpose.

There were larger rocks scattered about, one of which caught my attention. It had a flat surface with a back to it, like a stony armchair facing the sea. To test its comfort, I sat down on it looking out over the glittering, shifting water of the bay where the tide was receding and the waves came gently lapping against the shore. It was a soothing sound and I could have sat there for hours gazing out towards the distant horizon where the sea and sky mingled together, in one shimmering band of light.

It was Holmes who jolted me out of my reverie.

'Have you seen enough, my dear fellow?' he asked, 'only I thought it was time for lunch and after that I suggest we have a look round the church.'

The clean air had sharpened my appetite and I had no hesitation in agreeing with the first part of his suggestion. As for the church – well, I supposed grudgingly it was worth a visit since we were close to it.

The lunch at the Fisherman's Arms was certainly worth the climb up the steps and the walk along the cliff road that led to it. On the way we passed a tall iron gate behind which was a gravelled drive leading to Fulworth Hall, I supposed. The gate was padlocked and the house was shrouded in leaves, so that I saw no more of it than I had from the bay. Because of its concealed position, there was an air of mystery about the place that aroused my curiosity, as if it were hiding some secret. But remembering Holmes' dismissive attitude when I had spoken of it earlier, I said nothing to him about my reaction.

In complete contrast, the Fisherman's Arms had a lively, open atmosphere, full of noise and movement. Several customers were in the bar and I noticed that when we entered their conversations broke off and we were regarded with a slightly suspicious interest, as if we were intruders on their world, like foreigners from an unknown country.

However, it soon passed. The landlord evidently knew Holmes for he bustled forward to greet us and to conduct us to a table by the window.

'The usual, Mr Holmes?' he asked, and nodded to me, inviting me into his little circle.

Moments later the other customers resumed their conversations, also signalling we were accepted into their clan.

The lunch was excellent, consisting of cheese, home-made bread and pickles, and a large glass of local-brewed ale. Half an hour later, I sat back, replete with food and beer, sunshine and sea air.

'Ready for St Botolph's?' Holmes inquired and I agreed without hesitation for he seemed eager to show me round the features of his new environment, although I must admit I am no great admirer of country churches. They may look very handsome from the outside but their interiors strike me as being cold and damp, smelling of moist stone and mouldy plaster. They tend to put me in a melancholy mood and this one, St Botolph's, had that same effect on me when, having walked down the gravelled path that led to the porch, Holmes opened the door, releasing the first draught of moist, cold air from the interior of the building. Holmes seemed indifferent to it and went striding briskly ahead, leaving me to follow behind.

It was a large, bare building that seemed to exude an aura of death: from the memorial plaques fixed to the walls to the usual image of the crucifixion in the east window. It also seemed vast for its setting, designed to hold a large congregation although my impression of the area was of only a few scattered cottages here and there along the clifftops. Even the Fisherman's Arms was apparently unable to attract more than half a dozen customers while Fulworth Hall seemed empty of inhabitants.

It also seemed very old and from the little I knew about churches, dinned into me by my history teacher at school who had a penchant for ecclesiastical architecture, parts of it were probably Saxon. The rounded arches of the doorways and the plain, sturdy pillars suggested as much.

I pointed this out to Holmes who agreed with me. Evidently there were little booklets on sale by the door that contained a short history of the place. As for the size of the building, Holmes had an explanation for that too. In the past, Fulworth had been a thriving fishing community but over time the bay had silted up causing the fishing trade to decline and the population had shrunk with it to a point where the church could no longer support its own clergyman. The centre of the village had shifted to the next bay further along the coast where the conditions were better and it was the vicar from the new church of St Mary's who came every other Sunday to take communion and matins. Funerals were still held at St Botolph's and the very occasional wedding or baptism, many of the younger members of the population having moved to the newly established heart of the community. But even that had recently declined as a fishing centre, due to quite another drawback: the railway this time.

'Railway?' I asked, much surprised. 'But I thought the railways brought trade.'

'Not if they fail to come. Customers from the area had grown used to their fish being delivered within hours of it being caught. So when the railway line stopped short of Fulworth, possibly because it was too small to make the expense of extending it worthwhile, the fishing trade declined once again. A few of the more enterprising of the local inhabitants refused to be beaten and started up alternative businesses of their own: renting out bathing huts, for example, or taking visitors on little boating trips round the bay. Ask Maud Bellamy, if you're interested. Her father, Tom Bellamy, made a small fortune out of the holiday trade.'

As we stood talking, I became more and more aware of a draught round my ankles. That part of the chancel floor was composed of stone slabs covered by strips of coconut matting, leaving the edges exposed. It was from this area abutting the wall that the cold air was seeping and I shifted my feet trying to find a warmer place in which to stand.

Holmes broke off his explanation of the diminution of the population to ask, 'What on earth is the matter, Watson?'

'There is a dreadful draught coming up from the floor.' I replied. 'My feet are like ice!'

'Ah!' Holmes said softly, putting into the simple two-letter exclamation a wealth of meaning: surprise at my response, combined, I thought, with relief as if it were a remark he was hoping to hear.

'What do you suppose this draught signifies?' he continued.

'Signifies?' I repeated, unsure what he meant.

'What causes it, do you think?'

'Well,' I said uncertainly, 'I suppose there must be

a cellar of some sort under this part of the church.'

'A crypt perhaps?'

'It could be.'

'And when did you notice the draught?'

'Not long after I stepped onto this part of the floor.' I replied, wondering where this strange catechism was leading.

'Oh, well done, my dear fellow!' Holmes exclaimed. 'Not many people would have had the perspicacity to remark on it. And you are quite right. There is a vault under the church in exactly that position. In fact, it was partly for that reason why I wanted you to join me in Fulworth. There are some strange happenings going on here and it struck me that you would be the ideal companion to help me solve the mystery. You have that simple, down-to-earth attitude that is exactly what I need.'

I could have been offended by the remark for it suggested that I lacked imagination, a criticism he had once made about Inspector Lestrade, the Scotland Yard police officer with whom Holmes had collaborated during several investigations during our Baker Street days. It also suggested that he had invited me to Sussex not so much out of his friendship for me than for his own benefit. But no sooner had the thought crossed my mind than another arose to contradict it. He had *needed* my assistance and that was the greatest compliment he could pay me.

'What happenings are you referring to, Holmes? Are they connected with this business of the draught?'

'Come with me and I will show you exactly what I mean,' he replied and, turning on his heel, he strode back to the door through which we had entered. Much bemused, I followed him out into the graveyard where he set out purposefully, walking rapidly along a gravel path that led round to the back of the church, past the tower, to the far side of the building.

'Here we are,' he announced, coming to a halt and pointing to the base of the wall.

At first, I could not make out what he was indicating. The churchyard had been neglected and over the years grass and brambles had enveloped a stretch of earth that must have once been a small garden. A rose bush, half strangled by the overgrowth, pushed its head towards the light and the edge of the narrow strip of garden had been outlined with smooth, rounded stones probably taken from the beach.

Holmes was saying, 'There is another little garden directly opposite this one, just as overgrown and with a same edging of stones. When I first noticed it, I was intrigued, so I bent back the briars that were quite dense. In doing so, I uncovered three steps leading down to a low door set in the wall. It had one of those wrought-iron handles, shaped like a ring, such as you find on old buildings. Below it was a keyhole, also made of iron.

'My curiosity aroused, I bent the briars to one side so that I had easier access to the steps and, going gingerly down them, I was able to examine more closely the door and its lock and handle. Guess what I found Watson?'

It was a game Holmes loved to play with an unwitting participant and, knowing this, I decided not to fall for this old trick but to lie doggo, so to speak, and pretend total ignorance.

So I said, trying to look bewildered. 'I have no idea, Holmes. What was it?'

'Oil!' he replied triumphantly.

I was genuinely taken aback by this response.

'Oil?'

'Yes, my dear fellow, and plenty of it too. As well as the keyhole and the door handle, the hinges had also been liberally oiled and recently, which means, of course . . .'

He raised his eyebrows at me and this time the answer was so obvious that I was almost ashamed to reply.

'Someone was trying to break into the church, a thief no doubt, hoping to find silver candlesticks or something of value. Some church silverware is old and therefore of great interest to a collector.'

'Possibly, Watson, but why should he break into

the crypt and not into the church itself? But you could be right about the candlesticks. However, I think in this particular case, there was another motive.'

By this time, I was thoroughly roused by Holmes' remarks. There was an air of suppressed excitement about him that stimulated my own curiosity almost to a fever pitch of expectation.

'What motive?' I demanded eagerly.

'Hold your horses, Watson,' he replied. 'It is a complex story and one I think that should be told at leisure once we have seen what is in the crypt, which I suggest we examine later tonight after we have returned from our supper engagement at The Gables. For the time being, I propose we go back to the cottage and get ready for this evening. Mrs B will have gone by now so we shall have a clear run.'

Mrs B, as Holmes referred to her, had indeed departed by the time we returned to the cottage, leaving everything shipshape in her wake: beds made, breakfast things washed up and put away, rooms tidy and dusted. Whatever her drawbacks as a gossip, she was evidently an excellent housekeeper, a quality which Holmes readily admitted.

'You know, Watson,' he confessed, giving me a wry sideways look, 'I do appreciate her efficiency. In fact, I sometimes leave little thank-you notes or some small gift to make up for my negligent behaviour, although I do not think she feels offended about it anyway. She has come to the conclusion that I am eccentric and therefore anything I do is excusable. And what is more, I am a man and therefore any selfishness or inconsideration on my part is to be expected.'

As he spoke, I realised how much he had changed since the Baker Street days. That old Holmes would not have been so aware of other people's feelings, let alone apologise for them. It was a revelation that gave me great consolation and, later on, when I followed him around the garden on a tour of the beehives and listened to his enthusiastic account of the art of apiculture and the consequent delight of its delicious product, I felt even closer to Holmes. However, one small query still nagged away at the back of my mind: what on earth had he meant about the candlesticks in the crypt? It seemed to make no sense at all. Or was he merely suggesting that whoever had entered the crypt had come equipped with the means of lighting it? I could only suppose that later in the evening, when we investigated the place ourselves, he would explain this minor mystery.

CHAPTER THREE

I had mixed feelings about the invitation to the supper party at The Gables. Part of me was curious to meet Holmes' new friend, Harold Stackhurst; on the other hand, I felt a little uncertain about Holmes' relationship with him. Judging by the references Holmes had made now and again to Stackhurst in his letters to me, I gathered they met fairly frequently, for meals or walks or to go swimming together in the lagoons left behind in the bay when the tide went out. I was not exactly jealous of their friendship but I was aware that this new Holmes, the one I was getting used to, was a different person to the one I had known in London. He was much more relaxed and ready to socialise. The old Holmes had preferred his own company, living a solitary life in which I was on occasions his only contact with the outside world.

At the same time, I wondered what Stackhurst would make of me. Would he regard me as an interloper, someone from Holmes' past with whom he would rather not have to associate – although I realised this reaction was irrational. After all, the man had invited both of us to spend the evening with him, unless, of course, I was included out of mere politeness. Or perhaps curiosity, in the same way I was curious to meet him.

The invitation was for half past seven and, having spruced ourselves up, we set off for The Gables in the car in deference to our newly polished boots; to my relief, I must confess. Although I walked regularly in London and reckoned myself to be in a good state of health, I have to admit that my calves were still aching from our earlier expedition, particularly the long climb up and down the steps to the beach.

As soon as I drove up to The Gables and saw it was a large, Victorian building in the Gothic style, solid and conspicuous, its gables standing out against the skyline, I was not sure I liked it much. It was a little too pompous and extravagant for my taste and, as I parked the car, I wondered if Harold Stackhurst would share its characteristics.

Thank goodness, he did not. He was a pleasant,

frank-featured man, a bachelor in his forties, as Holmes had once described him, with a friendly smile as he greeted us at the door and welcomed us into the house.

As I had suspected, the Gothic style was a little too over-emphasised. The entrance hall and the staircase that led off it were panelled in dark oak that gave it a gloomy air although I was pleased to see no suits of armour, only a display of armorial shields that with their gold coronets were almost festive and cheered up the place.

A huge stained-glass window depicting more coronets and fabulous creatures, such as unicorns and griffins, illuminated the landing halfway up the stairs.

We were conducted into what I assumed was Stackhurst's private drawing room, a much more modest apartment furnished with sofas and chairs, where a decanter of sherry and glasses were waiting for us on a low table along with cigars and cigarettes should we want them.

I felt I ought to make some complimentary remark about the house. After all, it was Stackhurst's property and the place itself seemed to expect some expression of admiration. But to my relief, Stackhurst waved aside my remarks.

'Personally, I think it's hideous,' he replied, 'but it impresses my students and especially their parents who seem to think it's the height of good taste and architecture magnificence, better than Eton as one father expressed it. So it has its uses.'

'Who built it?' Holmes asked.

'A very foolish man called Henry Lovell, a self-made millionaire who wanted to impress his friends and colleagues. Unfortunately, he fell into the hands of a so-called architect who specialised in designing public houses. Anyway, to cut a long story short, he persuaded Lovell to build the house at an enormous cost on the top of the cliff, assuring him it would be an excellent investment. "Think of it!" he urged. "Sea views! Beautiful scenery! Beach parties!"

'Foolishly, he failed to mention the winter gales, the rocky coast that made sailing too dangerous and the fact that there was no easy access to the beach. So, after a season or two, Lovell's friends, or so he assumed them to be, made excuses not to join him on his clifftop mansion and having found himself alone among the stained-glass and the heraldic shields, he decided to sell. But no one seemed to share his taste for medieval fripperies and the price was gradually reduced until it reached a figure low enough for me to afford. So I bought the place and set up my establishment. I call it an academy in the brochures but, strictly speaking, its a crammer for students who need extra tuition for Civil Service examinations or applications for the army or navy.'

'And it has been successful?' Holmes suggested.

'Oh indeed it has!' Stackhurst responded warmly. 'My students are keen to pass their exams and I have been very lucky in building up an excellent teaching staff.'

At this point, he was interrupted by a peal on the front doorbell and he rose to his feet.

'Ah, that must be my other guests,' he said. 'If you will excuse me for a moment . . .'

He left the room, returning shortly with the new arrivals: a man in his thirties, accompanied by a young woman whom I recognised immediately from the photograph of her that had been pinned up in Holmes' darkroom. She lived up to the image I had seen there: the same clear-cut, delicate features, the same natural grace in the poise of her head and the same colouring that I had guessed from the black-and-white print. As I had imagined, her hair was a rich dark brown with gold and russet tints, such as you would find in autumnal foliage, while her eyes were like opals, mostly dark blue with flecks of green and gold in the pupils.

I was completely captivated by her beauty and by the aura of modesty and innocence about her, yet she seemed unaware of the effect she had on any man capable of normal reactions.

Her companion, I realised even before he was introduced to me, was Ian Murdoch, the mathematics tutor at The Gables. Holmes had mentioned him in one of his letters, not in a very complimentary manner, in which he had referred to the Lion's Mane inquiry and how Ian Murdoch had, for a time, been suspected of murdering Fitzroy McPherson, the science master at The Gables, until Holmes was able to prove his innocence.

Meeting him face-to-face, I could understand why he had aroused suspicion. He was a dark, thin, taciturn man, very tense, his eyes watchful and wary. He gave off an aura of powerful energy seething just below the surface, ready to boil over at the least provocation.

Also obvious were his feelings towards Maud Bellamy. Whenever he looked at her, his whole features softened and took on an expression of longing.

Even Holmes, despite his scorn of what he called the 'softer emotions', seemed touched by her although his attitude seemed one of affection. It was more the look an uncle might bestow on a favourite niece, not that of a lover.

As for Harold Stackhurst, I could not gauge his reaction to her. Having made the introductions, he had turned away to pour sherry for these new guests and I could not see his face apart from his profile and that expressed no more than the general cordiality of a good-natured host.

Despite these undercurrents of tension, it was an enjoyable evening. Stackhurst was an excellent host and, once we had been introduced, and the sherry, a good dry vintage, consumed, he conducted us into an adjoining dining room. A lavish supper had been laid out on a long table overlooking the rear garden of the house and a distant view of the Downs, shrouded now by the gathering twilight and the atmosphere of the party became more convivial. We helped ourselves informally to the various dishes of cold meats and cheeses, served with salads, and to the choice wines. It was at this point that Holmes introduced the subject of Fulworth Hall and its occupants, a topic that evidently intrigued others in the group. He had not so far referred to it in my presence but from his carefully casual tone I guessed it was of some importance to him.

'By the way,' he remarked, 'from time to time I have noticed a lady in widow's weeds walking along the beach. I think she lives in Fulworth Hall. Does anyone know who she might be?'

It was Ian Murdoch who answered him.

'Sorry, I can't help you,' he said, 'but I gather there's something of a mystery about the residents of Fulworth Hall.' Turning to Maud Bellamy, he added, 'You live locally, Maud. You're probably better informed than the rest of us. Do you know who she is?'

Maud Bellamy shook her head.

'I'm afraid I don't. I've heard people mention her but no one seems to know anything about her. Surely your housekeeper, Mrs Bagwell, will be able to help you, Mr Holmes? She was born in Fulworth and evidently knows everything about the place that is worth knowing. I advise you to ask her.'

Holmes darted a quick sideways glance at me, eyebrows raised and a small wry smile on his lips. It was gone in an instant and his face reassumed a pleasant, neutral expression.

'Of course!' he remarked, without a trace of irony in his voice. 'What a splendid idea!'

'She could probably tell you quite a lot about the smugglers as well,' Maud Bellamy continued.

'Smugglers!' Holmes repeated, his voice and manner changing to one of genuine eagerness.

Ian Murdoch took up the subject.

'Haven't you heard of them?' he asked. 'This stretch of coast used to be notorious for them. France is quite close and the caves in the cliffs were very useful for hiding contraband, brandy mostly, as well as tobacco and wine. The public house, the Fisherman's Arms, was also in on the game. They used to hide their goods in the cellar there, I'm told. Ask Reg Berry, the landlord. He'll show you where the contraband was concealed, in case the Excise men came searching.'

'Really?' Holmes sounded eager to know more about the smugglers and I could understand his curiosity. The information seemed to link up with the crypt in St Botolph's and the door that led into it; I wondered if Holmes had come to the same conclusion. I assumed he had.

Evidently it was a topic that sparked the interest of other members of the group and conversation passed on to further discussion about smuggling: how boats had put into the bay at the dead of night to unload their cargoes and how the smugglers with the aid of some of the local men had toiled up the steep path to the top of the cliffs with kegs of brandy on their shoulders and packets of tobacco rolled up in oilskins.

The conversation continued until eleven o'clock when Holmes rose to his feet, ready to take his leave, thanking Harold Stackhurst for the excellent supper and the fascinating company. He was keen, I thought, to set out on our own investigation of the church crypt, fired up no doubt by the talk of smugglers that had evidently caught his attention.

Turning to Maud Bellamy, he added, 'I understand you live in the village. Dr Watson has brought me here by car. May we offer to drive you home?'

Before she had the opportunity to reply, Ian Murdoch had stepped forward, his face flushed with anger, revealing the other side of his nature that I had suspected on first meeting him. There followed a moment of uneasy silence before Murdoch regained his composure, although there was still a hard edge to his voice when he replied.

'There is no need, Mr Holmes. I, too, have a car and I have already made arrangements to drive Miss Bellamy home.'

It was Maud Bellamy who smoothed over the awkwardness rather to my surprise; up to that point I had formed the impression that she was of an unassuming nature who would prefer to leave such decisions to the men rather than express her own preferences. Instead, in a clear, steady voice she addressed Holmes directly.

'Thank you very much, Mr Holmes, and you too, Dr Watson. It was most kind of you to make the offer that I would have been very pleased to accept. However, as Mr Murdoch has explained, he has already arranged to take me home.'

Then, glancing round at the four of us, at least three of whom were, I believe, more than a little attracted to her, she gave us all a charming smile before shaking hands all round.

Holmes and I left soon afterwards, after allowing enough time for Murdoch to drive away. His car had gone, I noticed, as Harold Stackhurst showed us out of the front door.

'A very pleasant evening,' I remarked as I turned

out of the drive and headed back towards Church Lane.

'I am very pleased you enjoyed it,' Holmes said. 'Stackhurst is an excellent host. Pity though, about Ian Murdoch. I thought he rather spoilt the last few minutes.'

It was said in a light-hearted manner but, having seen Murdoch's obvious possessive infatuation for Maud Bellamy, I was curious to know more about the man.

'I would imagine he has quite a temper when roused,' I remarked, adding as I remembered a detail from one of Holmes' letters, 'Wasn't he suspected of the murder of that other tutor at The Gables?'

'Fitzroy McPherson, you mean? Yes, Murdoch was thought to have killed him. His temper nearly lost him his post at The Gables as well. A little Airedale puppy belonging to McPherson annoyed him for some reason and he picked it up and threw it through a plate-glass window.'

'Oh, Holmes, how dreadful!' I exclaimed, deeply shocked by the information.

'I know. It was quite inexcusable. Harold Stackhurst was close to sacking him. It was only the fact that he was a good mathematics tutor that saved him. Incidentally, the dog survived but died later of grief, as we thought at the time, at the very same place that McPherson lost his life. But it was another victim of the *Cyanea capillata*, the jellyfish with the deadly sting.'

'There must have been a very strained relationship between the two men.'

'Apparently not,' Holmes corrected me. 'That particular incident of the dog blew over and they became quite close friends afterwards. In fact, Murdoch was very distressed by McPherson's death. No, it was quite a different situation that seemed to give Murdoch a motive for murder. You saw an example this evening.'

'You are speaking of Maud Bellamy?' I inquired.

We had reached Holmes' cottage and, having parked the car in the open space in front of the fruit trees and the row of beehives, I switched off the engine.

There was a silence before my old friend replied.

'Yes, you are right, Watson. Fitzroy McPherson and Maud Bellamy were secretly engaged to be married. After his death, we found a note from her in his pocket agreeing to meet him on the beach that very same evening. At the time, it was suspected that Ian Murdoch was also attracted to her. So it gave him a motive, as well as an opportunity to kill his rival, knowing when he would be on the beach.'

'But he wasn't arrested,' I pointed out.

'No, Maud Bellamy was adamant that Murdoch gave up all interest in her once he knew about the relationship between her and McPherson. She believed him as she knew the two men had become close friends.'

'And now?' I asked. 'What is their relationship since McPherson's death?'

I heard Holmes let out a deep breath but it was too dark to see his expression.

'That is indeed the question. Where exactly does their relationship stand now?'

I said bluntly, 'He is very possessive.'

'I know, Watson. Not a good basis on which to build a marriage, if that is what he has in mind. The only ray of hope is Maud Bellamy's strength of character. I do not think she would tolerate being dominated by anybody. She is very much her own person. I think you caught a glimpse of that side of her this evening. In the meantime, my dear fellow, there is nothing we can do but cross our fingers and hope for the best because the best she undoubtedly deserves.

'Now to turn to the other matter we planned for this evening: the crypt at St Botolph's. Perhaps that will take our minds off Ian Murdoch and his intentions towards Maud Bellamy. I suggest we walk to the church. It is much quieter than going in the car and I also recommend that we change into something more suitable for exploring an old crypt. By the way, did you bring the soft-soled shoes I mentioned in my letter?'

'Yes, Holmes. In fact, I bought them specially.'

I said it with a touch of irony, thinking: so that was why Holmes advised me to bring them. He had already decided to examine the crypt and had wanted me to be present when he did so; to what end I was not quite sure. As a witness? Or was it to serve again as a sounding board on which to try out his ideas?

'You are game?' Holmes inquired with an uncertain tone in his voice that I had never heard before and I hastened to assure him.

'Game? Of course I'm game, Holmes! When have I ever been otherwise?'

He laughed out loud as he slapped me on the shoulder.

'Good old Watson!' he cried. 'So let the chase begin!'

It took us less than a quarter of an hour to change into more suitable clothes for the night's expedition, Holmes returning from his room with two objects that he laid down on the table.

'Do you recognise either of these?' he asked.

I did indeed; in fact I recognised both of them. One was a bundle of metal rods of various sizes rolled up in a soft leather case, part of a first-class burglary kit. He had bought it during the investigation concerning Charles Augustus Milverton whose safe he broke into to retrieve certain letters that Milverton was using to blackmail one of Holmes' clients, Lady Eva

Brackwell. The rods were a set of picklocks, known among professional thieves as 'bettys'. Holmes had used them on several occasions and was quite an expert with them.

The other item was a small lantern called a 'bullseye', a pocket version of the type a policeman carries strapped to his belt as part of his equipment. A shutter could close off the light from the bullseye or focus the beam on any particular object that the officer wished to examine in more detail. Burglars also used them when they were 'cracking a crib', that is breaking into premises or a safe, say, after dark.

'So,' Holmes was saying, 'if you are ready to act as my colleague or, in this case I suppose "accomplice" would be a better word to use, shall we set off?'

'Ready for anything, Holmes,' I assured him.

'That's my Watson!' he exclaimed as we made for the door.

CHAPTER FOUR

It was quite dark when we set out on the twenty-minute walk to the end of the lane where it joined another narrow byroad that ran across the top of the cliffs, past the Fisherman's Arms, its windows dark. About a quarter of a mile further on, we reached the entrance to the grounds of Fulworth Hall, also in darkness, its gate closed.

A few minutes later, the silhouette of St Botolph's loomed to the left, dominating the horizon, the oblong of its tower obliterating part of the night sky.

The moon was clouded over so there was only the faint light of the stars to illuminate the scene, and the great mass of the sea had slipped away into the darkness apart from a pallid sheen that shifted restlessly to and fro. We could hear it, though: a deep breathing sound like that of a sleeping giant laid out at the foot of the cliffs.

By the time we had reached St Botolph's my eyes were becoming used to the darkness. So, too, were Holmes', I assumed, for he had no difficulty in finding the gate to the churchyard. Unlatching it, he set off at a brisk pace.

As far as possible we avoided the gravelled path and kept to the grass verge where our footsteps were inaudible. Indeed there were no sounds I could discern except for the gentle exhalations of the sea as it crept up the shore all those many feet below us. Even the wind was hushed as if it understood the need for silence.

A little further on we turned to the right, skirting round the bulk of the tower and, after a few more yards, we reached the place where the two small flower beds edged with stones marked the position of the steps leading down to the low wooden door set in the church wall. Holmes lit the little bullseye lantern and its beam illuminated an area big enough to confirm that the rose briars that Holmes had so carefully rearranged earlier in the day had not been disturbed. I heard him give a small sigh of relief and I felt my own muscles relax.

So far, so good. We had not yet been discovered.

'Keep *cave*, Watson,' Holmes murmured under

his breath and, as I turned away to face the path, I heard the faint clink of metal as Holmes opened the leather pouch and took out the picklocks. Hearing this, I risked a hurried glance over my shoulder and saw he was crouching down in front of the low door, inserting one of the rods into the keyhole by the narrow light of the lantern. It was apparently not the right one for the lock did not yield and it took several more attempts before I heard the wards give way at last and the door swing loose.

Risking another backward glance, I saw Holmes' face, his eyes glittering in triumph, as he eased the door fully open.

It was one of those occasions when one's senses are raised to a much higher pitch of awareness. Sounds were amplified and the sea no longer seemed to whisper but appeared to pound as the waves struck the shore. I could even smell it quite strongly: a salty tang mingled with the odour of seaweed and wet sand. But beneath these scents there was another aroma that at first I could not identify except it reminded me of the church; that same musty odour of damp stones and decaying plaster.

'Watson!' Holmes whispered urgently and I quickly transferred my attention to him. He was standing, shoulders hunched, in the low doorway, beckoning vigorously to me to join him.

The light from the little lantern, fluttering like a

pale moth as Holmes moved it to and fro, lit up the edges of the three steps leading downwards and I followed it gingerly, inch by inch, until I could feel a flat paved area in front of the door where Holmes was waiting. I joined him and the two of us shuffled forward, heads bent low, into the darkness beyond that seemed to be a black, floorless abyss, much to my alarm. And then, as my eyes adjusted to the gloom, I was able to pick out some details of our surroundings.

We were standing at the entrance of a low-ceilinged vault or crypt, floored with rough paving slabs in the centre of which was a large, oblong tomb like a stone dining table, the edges of its lid carved with an inscription that I could not decipher in the wavering light of the lantern. Before I had time to fix my eyes on it, the beam from the lamp had moved on. It passed rapidly over the rest of the interior and lit up walls that were lined with shelves, on which were resting what I thought at first to be several old wooden boxes until I suddenly realised they were coffins, each bearing a brass plate screwed to the lid.

However, it was the odour of decay that occupied my attention more than the contents of the crypt. It was so pungent that it seemed not only to fill my nostrils but also the bony cavities of my skull. It had even soaked into my hair and the pores of my skin so that I could smell it on my hands. It was a loathsome odour and for a few seconds I felt panic-stricken, desperate to get out of the place before the miasma of mortality suffocated me.

Holmes appeared to be unaffected. Lantern in hand, he was stooping low over the floor following some tracks in the dust, careful, I noticed, not to step on them and waving me back when I started to approach them. So I remained motionless, watching his movements and silently begging him to lead the way out of this sepulchre of shadows and old bones.

As if he had heard my silent plea, he turned and stepped back towards the door, motioning me to do likewise. I needed no encouragement. A few paces later and I was backing out through the doorway into the open air, which I gulped down like a drowning man coming to the surface.

I scrambled up the steps on my hands and knees, leaving Holmes to close and lock the door behind us.

'Are you all right, my dear fellow?' he asked with genuine concern, seeing me crouching there.

'Yes, Holmes; at least I think so.' I replied, struggling to my feet and trying to make my voice sound as normal as possible.

'Splendid!' came his reply. 'Then we shall set off for home.'

Pausing for only a few moments, he turned the lantern's beam towards the steps while he bent the rose briars back into place. That done to his satisfaction, he started off the way we had come, through the churchyard and down the lane to his cottage, striding along so fast that I had difficulty in keeping up with him. Once inside the house, he lit the lamps and drew the curtains over the window before pouring both of us a glass of whisky and soda. I accepted mine gratefully.

The walk and the fresh air had cleared my head of any lingering effects of the putrid odour in the crypt and I was ready now to confront Holmes, a challenge he seemed aware of, for he looked across at me directly, his eyes very bright and searching.

'I know exactly what you are going to say, Watson,' he began. 'I invite you down here for a holiday by the sea and then involve you in a situation that you do not understand and which I make no effort to explain. No, please do not say anything, my dear fellow, just oblige me by sitting there and finishing your whisky.'

I did as I was told. There was no gainsaying Holmes when he was in one of his masterful moods.

'I admit I invited you here not entirely for unselfish motives,' he continued. 'If you remember you once referred to yourself as the "whetstone" for my mind. It was an unusual but perceptive simile. I do indeed need your presence to sharpen my own mental processes. I think more clearly when I have someone else to whom I can express my thoughts. And I still do. So let me start again, my old friend, and explain my reasons for inviting you here. You remember the walk we took along the beach?'

'Yes, very clearly,' I replied. As we seemed to have reached a point in which honesty was to be the touchstone of our conversation, I decided to follow his example and speak my own mind. So I continued, 'To be frank, Holmes, at the time I felt there was some other motive behind that walk.'

'Really?' Holmes seemed astonished. 'How perspicacious of you! There was indeed another reason. Although I genuinely wanted to introduce you to my new surroundings, I also wished you to see the setting of a strange sequence of events. It was this that persuaded me to send for you in the first place. You remember that large, flat rock on the left of the beach?'

'Indeed I do. In fact, I sat on it. It was like an armchair made of stone but comfortable all the same and with a wonderful view of the sea.'

'Good! Now let me explain its significance. About three weeks before you came, I was walking along the clifftop path overlooking the cove. For some reason, I had found it difficult to sleep that night so at about one o'clock I got up, dressed and went for a walk, thinking it might help me settle down. I reached a point on the cliff path where there is a gap in the hedge and from where one has an uninterrupted view of the cove and I stopped to admire it.

'It was a clear night and there was no difficulty in picking out the details of the shoreline. While I was looking, I saw a figure crossing the beach to that flat rock and sitting down on it. It was quite obviously a woman who was dressed in a long black cloak that was hooded so I could not see her features, but I could make out certain details of her appearance. She was of medium height and build, not young but not old either for she held herself upright and walked easily. I was mystified by her presence there on the beach for she seemed to do nothing but sit there looking out to sea.'

'But, Holmes!' I protested, thinking that, unusually for him, he was making far more of the situation than it warranted. 'Perhaps like you she couldn't sleep and had decided to go for a walk.'

'Of course that was my first thought,' Holmes corrected me. 'But that does not explain what happened later. So pray, allow me to continue. The following night I still could not sleep, so I went out again for a stroll. To be honest, the mysterious lady in black was still very much in my mind. Who was she? Where had she come from? What was she doing there? I was therefore oddly relieved to see her again, sitting on the same rock and looking out to sea just as she had done the night before, only this time there was a change in the circumstances. You remember that flight of steps on the far side of the cove?'

'Those you said led down from Fulworth Hall and were private?'

'Exactly so. Well, as I stood there looking out over the cove, a man came hurrying down those steps and ran across the beach towards the woman. As soon as I saw him, I drew back behind the hedge so, should he glance up, he would not see me.'

'And?' I prompted him, curious now to hear the full story.

'He bent down over the woman and was obviously trying to persuade her to get up and go with him, all the time glancing around to make sure no one was watching. This went on for several minutes until at last she seemed to agree for she stood up and, taking his arm, allowed him to lead her across the beach and up the steps. At the top, the pair of them disappeared behind the shrubs in the garden so I did not see exactly where they went after that.'

'To Fulworth Hall?' I suggested.

'That was my conclusion. So I assumed that is where she must live, but that is only part of the answer to the puzzle. I still do not know her name nor who the man is nor what connection they both have to Fulworth Hall.'

'What sort of man was he?'

'Middle-aged, short, stockily built. Judging by

the way he spoke to the woman, he was a servant of some kind.'

'A butler?'

'No, not distinguished enough for that. I would suggest a gardener or a handyman. But he seemed very solicitous towards our lady in black, as if she were a child or an invalid. Whoever he is though, that still does not explain the matter of the crypt.'

Something about his tone of voice prompted me to ask, 'You think they may be connected?'

Instead of replying directly, Holmes got to his feet and crossing to his desk, took out a slim pamphlet, which he handed to me.

'Read that, Watson,' he said, 'and tell me what you make of it.'

It was one of the booklets, priced sixpence, which I had noticed on a rack just inside the door of St Botolph's together with a wooden box for contributions. Flicking over the pages, I noticed briefly that the contents covered a general history of the church, including a reference to its Saxon origins, together with a list of the clerics who over the generations had served as rectors of the parish.

'Page fourteen!' Holmes instructed me, watching me with a curiously intent gaze.

Page fourteen, I discovered, was devoted to an account of a local family, the Trevalyans, who it seemed were regarded almost as Lords of the Manor.

Originally from Cornwall, it stated; made their money from tin mining; one of the younger sons, Henry, had moved to Fulworth at the turn of the century. It was he who had the original Fulworth Hall, a Jacobean house, pulled down and had the present building erected in its place.

There followed a brief account of the Trevalyan family history up to the year 1901, the date when the booklet was published. Henry, it stated, had married and produced two sons, George, the eldest, and a younger son, Charles, who had died in childhood. In his turn, George also married but in his case had only one son, Henry, presumably named after his grandfather. There were two daughters, both of whom had died young.

The second Henry Trevalyan's progeny was even more limited to a daughter, christened Henrietta, perhaps a token reference to the non-existent son who would have carried on the family tradition of nomination. There was no further mention of this daughter. Perhaps like her uncle, Charles Trevalyan, and his two anonymous sisters she, too, had died young.

Brief though it was, this genealogical record struck me as tragic. Like the gradual decay of the original Fulworth village, from a thriving Saxon settlement with its imposing church to mere scattering of cottages, the Trevalyans had also dwindled away to the last Henry who had died in 1898, ten years earlier, apparently leaving no one to carry on his bloodline, his once elegant home, Fulworth Hall, slowly disintegrating on the clifftop.

There was another relic mentioned in the last paragraph – the family tomb installed in the crypt of St Botolph's where Henry Trevalyan had been laid to rest among his deceased ancestors, the last of the lineage.

'You see the connection?' Holmes asked, as I closed the booklet and laid it down on the table. 'There seems to be a link with the Trevalyan family that could suggest the likelihood that whoever oiled the lock and entered the crypt had access to it; a key in other words.'

'But according to this,' I protested, tapping the booklet, 'the family died out with the death of the last Henry Trevalyan who left no heir to carry on the bloodline.'

'Apparently so,' Holmes agreed but not very positively. 'But I feel there is more missing information that we must inquire into. Do you recall the conversation we had with Maud Bellamy?'

'Yes I do, but I do not see—'

'She recommended a person who knows about local history,' Holmes continued brushing aside my intervention.

'Did she?' I asked, having forgotten to whom he was referring.

'Someone who was born and brought up in Fulworth.'

The penny suddenly dropped much to my astonishment.

'You mean Mrs B, Holmes?'

Holmes gave me a wry smile and nodded.

'But I thought you were doing your best to avoid her?'

'So I was. But the time has come for a change in tactics, and as quickly as possible. I suggest we start tomorrow morning without delay. So prepare yourself to listen to her medical complaints and look sympathetic. Some palliative remedy in the form of a pill or lotion would also do very nicely. I suggest you rummage around in that doctor's bag of yours, my dear fellow, and come up with some physic for a stiff neck. I do not think you will need any medication for loosening the tongue.'

However, before my meeting with Mrs B, another situation arose that occupied my attention and caused me more concern.

It was that same night and at about midnight when I was awakened by the sound of Holmes' bedroom door opening and footsteps softly descending the stairs. Moments later, the front door opened and closed. Holmes, for it could be no one else, had left the house but for what reason I could not immediately understand.

A sudden illness, I wondered. Or was he experiencing one of those bouts of sleeplessness that he had referred to earlier in the evening during which, he had walked along the cliffs overlooking the cove and seen for the first time the Lady in Black seated on a rock and looking out to sea?

Fully awake now and curious to better understand the rather puzzling circumstances for Holmes' night-time excursion, I got out of bed and, putting on my dressing gown, I followed his example and went downstairs also to let myself out of the front door.

The moon was bright, the sky cloudless, and, like Holmes in his earlier outing, I found no difficulty in picking out details of my surroundings. But although I had a good view of the lane that led up to the clifftop and the hedges that lined it, I could only catch a glimpse of Holmes' tall, lean figure walking rapidly ahead of me.

More curious than ever, I hurried after him, when suddenly he disappeared. Another mystery but a minor one in this case for, once I reached the point where he had vanished, I found the gap in the hedge which he had mentioned in his account of his previous midnight ramble and, like him, discovered the uninterrupted views of the cove below.

It was a breathtaking scene: a great sweeping vista of the beach and beyond it, the sea on which the moonlight fell in a sheen of silver that tumbled as the waves gently lapped the shore. Then the beach itself, empty of everything except for pale sand and the dark shapes of the rocks that rose out of it like strange sea creatures washed ashore.

There was no sign yet of Holmes, although there was no mystery attached to this. From my own experience of climbing down the steps to the cove earlier, I remembered it took several minutes to make the descent, longer if one was going up, and that the contours of the cliff hid the path until one had nearly reached its foot, and, indeed moments later, Holmes' figure emerged and began to walk across the open sand.

As he had told me, he had crouched back into the cover of the hedge when he had first seen the Lady in Black so that his presence would not be noticed, and I did exactly the same. But Holmes never once looked up, not even when he reached the large flat rock on which she had sat. Holmes seated himself on it as she had done, his head turned towards the sea, his back to the cliffs, and there he remained, unmoving, for the next half an hour or so at which point, I gave up my vigil and quietly retreated back along to the lane and to the cottage where I went back to my bed.

However, I did not sleep but lay awake listening for Holmes' return, and thinking over the night's experiences, for they puzzled me greatly, one aspect in particular. It was now quite clear that Holmes' interest in the Lady in Black was much more than mere curiosity but what else it was I could not understand. I was also convinced that my role in this was more complex than had first appeared, although that also remained uncertain. Nevertheless one condition was obvious. I would have to put all this to the back of my mind until Holmes was ready to confide in me completely.

It was half past two in the morning before I heard Holmes let himself into the cottage and his bedroom door close. It was then that I finally allowed myself to go to sleep, remembering that Mrs B was due to arrive the next morning and I had better get some rest before she came.

CHAPTER FIVE

Mrs B arrived promptly at ten o'clock the following morning, her appointed hour and, curious to see Holmes' housekeeper for the first time, I loitered near the sitting room window so that I could catch a glimpse of her before meeting her face-to-face.

From the few facts that Holmes had told me about her – that she was a widow, a good, plain cook and thorough in her work but too garrulous for his taste – I had imagined her to be, for no good reason, a large lady of a domineering nature whose late husband had been firmly kept under her thumb.

In fact, she was the antithesis of my expectations.

She was a small, thin, grey-haired woman for whom the best descriptive word to sum her up was 'taut'. She seemed to emit a suppressed energy that was almost palpable, like an electric charge. That was obvious from my very first sight of her in the brisk efficiency with which she wheeled her bicycle, the old-fashioned sit-up-and-beg type, into the garden where she propped it up against the outbuilding that housed Holmes' beekeeping paraphernalia. It was done in the most energetic manner, as if she were making sure that the bicycle, along with the shed itself, was aware of her dominance over both of them. That finished with, she set off towards the cottage, first lifting out of the large wicker basket strapped to the handlebars a neatly rolled bundle that I discovered afterwards contained an all-enveloping pinafore of a blue-chequered pattern and a pair of comfortable house shoes, both of which she donned as soon as she entered the house. However, oddly enough, she retained her hat, a black felt article not unlike an upturned basin, bound round with purple ribbon and topped off with a bunch of artificial violets that added an unexpected festive air to her appearance.

The previous evening Holmes and I had discussed the best strategy to use in persuading her to tell us all she knew about the Trevalyans, although Holmes was quite positive that very little effort would be needed. It was simply a matter of finding the right nudge, so to speak, to get her started: her health, in other words. To that end, it was decided I would introduce the subject immediately by offering her my sympathy and some ameliorative medication.

The first piece of advice was easy to carry out. As a doctor, I had among my patients several elderly ladies like Mrs B, who suffered from a whole catalogue of ailments and who needed no more than a sympathetic ear to restore their well-being. Unfortunately, in Mrs B's case, she would have had little or no commiseration from Holmes, his ear not being tuned to such appeals.

The second piece of advice was more difficult to fulfil. Although I had my medical bag with me, perhaps rather foolishly feeling incomplete without it, I had assumed I was going on holiday on the Sussex coast and that all the medical needs that might be called for would be minor injuries, such as cuts and grazes resulting from rock climbing. Therefore, I had brought little more than bandages and iodoform with me.

I decided that the best approach with Mrs B was a direct one, so as soon as I had been introduced to her by Holmes who, I noticed, put a special emphasis on the word 'doctor', I plunged straight in.

'I am sorry to hear from Mr Holmes that you have a stiff neck,' I said, using my best bedside manner, to which she responded immediately, first casting a grateful, if astonished, glance in Holmes' direction. 'How did that come about?'

'Turning mattresses,' she replied promptly.

'Then we must put a stop to that for the time being,' I advised, thinking that Holmes deserved some punishment for his lack of sympathy for Mrs B's malady, trivial though it might seem, even if it were only a minor penalty of suffering the discomfort of a lumpy mattress for a fortnight or so.

Holmes took the point for he gave me a nod and a wry smile of recognition, a private communication to which I replied with a nod and a smile of my own.

Mrs B was acute enough to realise that some silent dialogue or other was taking place between the two of us but could not, of course, interpret it and I hastened to fill the gap before it lengthened and became embarrassing.

So I continued as planned.

'Come and sit down at the table, Mrs Bagwell,' I began. 'I am going to put a hot compress on your neck, in my experience as a doctor, the best remedy for a strained muscle.'

At this cue, part of the strategy that we had decided on the previous evening, Holmes drew out a chair at the table and I went to the kitchen to collect the towel that was already soaking in a bowl of hot water, ready for use. Wringing it out, I carefully wrapped it around Mrs B's neck who was by now quite relaxed and visibly delighted by the attention she was receiving.

Holmes and I joined her at the table and the session we had planned began.

'Now, Mrs Bagwell,' I said, 'while we wait for the hot compress to take effect, I wondered if you could help me with some information I need to complete a little inquiry I am making.'

Mrs B looked even more delighted at this request for it placed her again in the unusual but gratifying position of being in the centre of attention.

'I'll do my best, Dr Watson,' she replied. 'What's your inquiry about, sir?'

'It concerns a special interest of mine: genealogy.'

Seeing an expression of uncertainty pass over her face, I realised my mistake and hurried to correct it.

'Family history,' I explained. 'It is the Trevalyans I am curious about. The other day I read a little booklet about the church and the Trevalyan family was mentioned.'

That part of our scheme was, at least, true, I told myself. The next, however, was entirely false and I felt uncomfortable at using it. But it was in a good cause and with that excuse in my mind, I pressed on with my deception.

'You see,' I continued, mentally crossing over my fingers, a gesture I used to make as a child to protect myself against any retribution that might befall me for telling a fib, 'Trevalyan is one of my family's names. I have an aunt who is a Trevalyan, at least she married one, and I was wondering if there was any connection.'

Mrs B seemed fascinated by the idea.

'A Trevalyan!' she repeated. 'Well, I suppose she could have married one of the family.'

'Tell me about them,' I suggested.

'They were nice enough, I suppose, especially Mrs Trevalyan. As for the husband, Henry, he wasn't liked as much in the village as her.'

'You knew him? What sort of a person was he?'

It was Holmes who asked these questions.

'A hard man,' Mrs B responded. 'Very much the boss, or so he liked to think.'

There was no hesitation in her voice now and her whole face had brightened up while her eyes were alert and busy, glancing to and fro between the two of us. It was evidently a topic she had strong feelings about.

Without any further coaxing on our part, she continued, 'He died about ten years ago. Now that was a big event in the village. The bells were rung and the kiddies had the day off from school. And the carriages! There must have been ten of them, all draped in black and the horses had black plumes on their heads. It was quite a to-do, I can tell you. You'd think he was royalty the fuss that was made. As for the wreaths, well, they were piled up on that tomb he had built in the crypt with the family name carved round the lid. Not a bit like his wife. She was quite different. I used to wonder sometimes how she put up with him.'

'He sounds a difficult man.' Holmes commented.

'Stuck up,' Mrs B responded in a decisive tone, as if the two words summed him up and there was no more to be said about him.

'Did they have any children?' I asked.

The question had an unexpected effect on Mrs B. The triumphant air she had assumed in speaking of her memory of Henry Trevalyan immediately vanished to be replaced by a reserved, almost apologetic manner. For several long moments there was silence in which Holmes and I regarded her, eyebrows raised in anticipation. But, as we had expected, the need to talk overrode all other considerations.

'Well,' she began, drawing in a deep breath, 'as you know I'm not the one to pass on tittle-tattle or to speak ill of the dead, but there was one child, a girl, Henrietta, or Hetty, as everyone called her.'

She seemed to run out of steam for she halted and looked at both of us, as if trying to judge our reaction to whatever she had to say. I caught her glance and nodded to her encouragingly. It seemed to work for she continued.

'She was lovely as a child, a pretty little thing. Mrs Trevalyan used to ask some of the children from the village up to the house for her birthday parties.

Lovely, they were: balloons and jelly and someone to entertain the kiddies after tea. And then suddenly it stopped. Hetty was nearly eighteen by then and it was put about she was too old for birthday parties. She was going to school at a posh place in Lewes as a weekly boarder. But she left there; some said she'd been – what's the word? – ex . . . ?'

'Expelled?' Holmes suggested.

'Yes, that's the one I was looking for. Chucked out, in other words.'

'Why?' Holmes asked.

To my relief, she turned to Holmes.

'What do you expect? The usual trouble. Men!'

'Men!' Holmes and I exclaimed simultaneously.

Mrs B hurried to correct herself.

'Well, one man; someone she met in Lewes, on holiday there, or so I've been told. Anyway, she ran off with him.'

'Where to?' Holmes asked.

Mrs B shrugged.

'Somewhere up north, I believe.'

'Did they marry?' I asked.

'That I can't tell you,' Mrs B replied, 'all I know is she left and no one has seen anything of her since. It's as if she disappeared off the face of the earth. It put an end to life at the Hall I can tell you. There were no more tea parties or Christmas treats as there used to be. In the past, the family had joined in the village dos, at least Mrs Trevelyan did. She always handed out the prizes at the flower shows or she'd call round on the old people with a basket of groceries. She was a real lady, she was. One of the Lockharts from Barton, highly respected; the family had been farming the same land for generations. But after the scandal over Hetty, all that giving parties and going out helping other people stopped. Neither of them ever showed their face in the village again. Mind you, I blamed *him* for all that. It was such a scandal, you see. They said he'd cut Hetty off without a penny and wouldn't even have her name mentioned. Then he died.'

The last sentence was said with more than a touch of *schadenfreude* and I had the feeling that Mrs B added to it a silent addendum of 'And serves him right!'

But Mrs B had not quite finished.

'You can understand why she asked to be buried in her own village, not in the crypt. You can't blame her, poor woman. I wouldn't want to share a grave with *him*.'

The remark served to round off the conversation and even Mrs B seemed to realise it had, literally, come to a dead end. Looking embarrassed she began to unwind the towel from around her neck.

'Thank you, Dr Watson. The stiffness has almost gone, so I'd better get on. There's the washing-up to do and the beds to make.'

'Then we shall get out of your way.' Holmes replied. 'Are you ready, Watson? We have that appointment in Lewes this morning.'

'Do we?' I asked. It was the first time I had heard of it. Holmes gave me a withering glance as he rose from the table and I hurriedly tried to cover up my gaffe.

'Of course,' I mumbled. 'Sorry, I'd forgotten all about it.' However, as we left the room I could not resist a last thrust of my own at Holmes. Turning back to Mrs B, I said in my best professional voice, 'Don't forget my advice about not turning mattresses,' relieved that she had not asked for any medication after all.

I picked him up over the matter of this supposed assignation as we were getting into the car.

'What appointment?' I demanded.

His reply was quite astonishing.

'With Langdale Pike.'

Langdale Pike, I should explain, was one of Holmes' old contacts from his Baker Street days. A strange, indolent character, he spent most of his time sitting in the bow window of his club in St James' Street, collecting up the tittle-tattle of the latest scandals amongst the members of high society for the gossip column he wrote for what Holmes described as the 'garbage' newspapers. So, in many ways, he was not unlike a female version of Mrs B only with a better class of subject matter.

However, it was said that he earned a good income from his journalism. In the past, Holmes had occasionally consulted him when he needed some background information, as in the Three Gables case, rewarding Pike with scraps of gossip he had picked up during his investigations. His professional title, Langdale Pike, was obviously a *nom de plume*, borrowed from the name of the Westmorland Hills, the Langdale Pikes.

I was much taken aback when Holmes spoke of him.

'Pike?' I reiterated as I started the car. 'Good heavens! Is he still alive?'

'I hope so. I am proposing to send a telegram to his club from Lewes. I hate to think it might be wasted.'

'Why from Lewes? Why not the post office in Fulworth?'

'Because there are too many ears and eyes in the village. Before one can snap one's fingers, the contents of my telegram will be common knowledge. It would not surprise me if Mrs B knew all about it by tomorrow morning.'

'But what on earth can Pike do in this case? I thought it was high society he was interested in?'

'So it is. But any scrap of gossip can whet his appetite. Like that character in Shakespeare, he is a "snapper-up of unconsidered trifles". According to Mrs B, herself a "snapper-up", there was that scandal in the Trevalyan family, bad enough, at least in Henry Trevalyan's eyes, to cause him to disinherit his daughter. If anyone can ferret out the truth, Langdale Pike will do so.'

It was said with such certainty that I fell silent.

'I thought,' Holmes continued, briskly changing the subject, 'that we might stop for coffee in Lewes. I believe the Rose and Crown hotel has a good reputation.'

For the rest of the journey, Holmes, who seemed to be in a jocular mood, chatted about a variety of subjects from Elizabethan comedies to the fascination of beekeeping, and the subject of Langdale Pike was dropped for the time being.

Holmes spent at least twenty minutes in Lewes' post office, so I assumed the telegram he was sending to Langdale Pike must be a long one. However, it was evidently only part of his errand for when eventually he emerged, I noticed he was carrying a newspaper under his arm, which he seemed to have folded back to a particular page, and when we had seated ourselves in the Rose and Crown, he placed it on the table, as if he wished to draw my attention to it. It was a copy of the local *Lewes Gazette* and the page that lay uppermost bore in large print the headline, *THEFT AT MELCHETT MANOR* with below it in smaller typeface, *Police Seek Gang of Thieves*.

Holmes tapped the column with his long index

finger, indicating I was to peruse it. I did so and it read as follows:

Police were called to Lower Melchett Manor in the early hours of Wednesday morning to investigate a burglary during which several items of silver were stolen. The owners, Sir Oliver and Lady Wayne, were not in residence at the time and were unaware of the theft until their butler telegraphed them in Italy. They should be returning to England in the near future. The investigation of the burglary is being conducted by Inspector Bardle of the Sussex Constabulary.

I looked across at Holmes.

'Inspector Bardle!' I exclaimed. 'Isn't it the same policeman who investigated that case involving Fitzroy McPherson?'

'Yes, that's the one!'

'I remember you referred to it in a letter you wrote to me about the case. You seemed to take to the inspector despite his rather slow country ways.'

'Indeed, I found him a decent, honest fellow,' Holmes agreed. 'Perhaps a little too eager to keep to the well-trodden path, like a lot of policeman, rather than striking out on his own. Would you like to meet him?'

'You mean—?'

'By taking a trip to Lower Melchett? Is that what you were going to say? What a wonderful idea, Watson! We could call on Inspector Bardle at the Manor for old time's sake. Besides, it is a very pleasant drive there.'

There was a mischievous air about him that I could not quite account for and it was in the same teasing manner that he took something from his pocket and laid it down on the *Lewes Gazette*. It was a small object that was difficult to identify, made of metal with a silvery sheen to it and appeared to have a tiny handle, bent in half, to one end of which was attached a rounded head, flattened into a squashed irregular shape.

'Now what do you make of that, my dear fellow?' he asked, his eyes twinkling.

'I have no idea.' I replied.

'Then let me give you a clue. I found it on the steps leading down to the crypt at St Botolph's. You were keeping *cave* so probably did not notice it. It was hidden under the foliage of that rose briar. Still no idea, Watson? Then what about another clue? The shapes in the dust. Does that help?'

'Not at all,' I said, a little huffily, as I was getting rather tired of the game.

'In that case, I suggest we leave the puzzle for the time being and make our way to Lower Melchett. By the way, I would rather you did not mention any of this to Inspector Bardle. It is still a very young idea on my part; newly hatched and not yet ready to fly.'

And with that, he left the hotel and, as I followed after him, I wondered what on earth it all meant. Shapes in the dust? A small metal object that looked as if it had been trodden on? I would certainly not confide any of it to Inspector Bardle. It made no sense at all.

Instead, I decided to follow Holmes wherever he led and trust that eventually these riddles would be solved.

CHAPTER SIX

Holmes was right; it was indeed a pleasant drive to Lower Melchett through scenery quite different to that of Fulworth. There were no cliffs, no sudden glimpses of the sea nor distant views of the Downs. Instead these were replaced by the softer undulating contours of farmland and meadows where sheep grazed or cottages were clustered together in leafy settlements.

Lower Melchett was one of these, a pretty rural village evidently cherished by its inhabitants judging by the carefully tended gardens and the profusion of window boxes and hanging baskets overflowing with flowers.

There was a small shop in the centre of the

village, like the houses bedecked with blooms, and a few yards beyond it the local inn, The Wheatsheaf, according to the sign, by the roadside.

'Pull in here!' Holmes suddenly ordered, taking me by surprise. It was too early for lunchtime, I thought. Nevertheless I obeyed and turned on to the gravelled forecourt of the inn where I parked the car.

'I shan't be long,' Holmes promised as he scrambled quickly out of the passenger seat and set off at a brisk pace for the door of the tavern, ducking his head to avoid a hanging basket of pink and blue flowers.

So something was afoot, I surmised, although quite what I was not exactly sure, except it had something to do with the burglary at Melchett Manor and Inspector Bardle's involvement with it, even though I could not discern its connection, if any, to the Lady in Black inquiry.

Before I had time to follow this train of thought any further, Holmes was back, tapping on the window and urging me to find a better place to park.

'I've booked a table for two for luncheon and the landlord has said we may leave the car here for the time being,' he said.

At this point I gave up trying to puzzle out Holmes' intentions. It was better, I decided, to follow his instructions and postpone the questions until later. So I started the car and eased it forward to a space on the far side of the forecourt where Holmes joined me. I gathered from his gestures that he wanted me to follow him across the inn's yard to the far side of the road.

'Where are we going now, Holmes?' I asked, assuming he would reply: 'To Melchett Manor of course, to meet Inspector Bardle,' as I could see what I took to be the entrance gates to the Manor a little further down the road on the right. But instead of turning in that direction, Holmes crossed the road to the other side where there was a gap in the hedge beside which stood a white-painted fingerpost marked 'Public Footpath'.

'I thought,' Holmes remarked as he climbed over the stile, 'that a little stroll to stretch our legs would do us good.'

A little stroll indeed! I thought but I said nothing. Judging by the smile he gave me, he was in one of his jocular moods and it was better not to rise to his bait. So I followed him over the stile where we found ourselves in a large meadow edged with trees, beyond which I caught a glimpse of chimneys and the sloping roof of a house: Melchett Manor, I surmised, a conjecture that appeared to be correct for Holmes suddenly left the path and cut across the field towards it, with me still following in his wake.

A few minutes later we had reached the far side and were pushing through the leafy hedge. There was, however, a final obstacle to be crossed: an iron fence which we clambered over to find we were faced with a sign as solid and as forbidding as a policeman or, in this case more appropriately a gamekeeper: a large noticeboard bearing in black paint the words,

MELCHETT MANOR. PRIVATE PROPERTY. TRESPASSERS WILL BE PROSECUTED.

I took a quick sideways glance at Holmes to gauge his reaction but he showed none. Calmly brushing leaves and pieces of broken twigs from his clothes, he set off walking briskly up the driveway towards a house, which could only be Melchett Manor and which seconds later emerged fully into view through the foliage to stand, grand and elegant, before us.

She – and the use of the feminine pronoun seemed totally relevant, for the house resembled a refined, aristocratic lady dressed for some fashionable occasion – was in the same Regency style as Fulworth Hall but compared to this house, the Hall with its overgrown gardens and general air of neglect, seemed like a poor relation. Here the stucco was dazzlingly white and the glass in the tiers of the windows set in the façade glittered in the sunshine.

'Holmes,' I began but remembering my decision to follow where he led, I kept silent and fell in behind him as he climbed the steps of the pillared portico and pressed the doorbell; not an ordinary bell push, nothing as mundane as that, but a circlet of polished brass in which a white china button was embedded like a large, lustrous pearl.

We heard the bell ring twice inside the hall and moments later the door was opened by a tall, superior-looking butler who announced even before Holmes had a chance to speak, 'The Manor is closed today to all visitors, sir.'

He seemed about to shut the door but Holmes prevented him by laying his hand against the frame.

'I have a message for Inspector Bardle. Would you please make sure he receives it immediately?' he requested, handing over one of his visiting cards, which he produced from his inner pocket and the butler perused it quickly.

He was too well trained to show any reaction to the name on the card, not even a raised eyebrow but he was evidently impressed by it for he stood aside to let us in.

'If you would please wait here, gentleman,' he said. 'I will make sure the inspector receives your card at once.'

And with that, he bowed briefly and crossing the hall, began to mount the staircase, passing a uniformed police officer who was standing at its foot, looking uncomfortably out of place in his sombre uniform and heavy boots in the elegant setting of gilt-framed mirrors, antique furniture and silk draperies of Melchett Manor's entrance hall.

'What is going on, Holmes?' I asked *sotte voce* but all I got in reply was a little smile and a laconic, 'Wait and see, my dear fellow,' before he turned away to inspect with fastidious attention a marble bust of a beautiful young lady displayed on a nearby cabinet.

So I gave up and keeping to my decision to follow where he led, I fell silent and waited.

I had not long to wait. Hardly two minutes later footsteps were heard crossing the upper landing and the burly figure of a man in civilian clothes, beaming broadly, came hurrying down the stairs, already holding out a hand to greet Holmes who stepped forward, his own hand at the ready, both men obviously delighted to meet one another.

'Mr Holmes!' declared the inspector.

'Inspector Bardle!' exclaimed Holmes in unison.

Their voices mingled in the shared greetings and both laughed out loud at the vocal duet, Inspector Bardle slapping Holmes on the shoulder with his free hand to emphasise his delight at the encounter.

'Allow me to introduce Dr Watson, an old colleague of mine,' Holmes continued. 'And this, Watson, is Inspector Bardle of the Sussex Constabulary whose acquaintance I made during the Lion's Mane inquiry.'

'A pleasure to meet you, Dr Watson,' the inspector said, shaking me by the hand. 'Mr Holmes mentioned you several times during that case. He spoke of you as his chronicler and I think he missed your company.'

I was momentarily lost for words by his frankness and by my first impression of him. He was not at all what I had expected. A stolid, middle-aged man, he had the bovine features of a friendly cow who stood four-square on the ground as if rooted there, regarding me with large, dark, speculative eyes as he took my hand.

'Is it possible to go somewhere quiet where we are not likely to be disturbed?' Holmes was saying as this little exchange of greetings was completed.

Bardle showed no surprise at this request, merely remarking, 'Of course, Mr Holmes, I'll have a word with the butler to make sure we're left alone. If you'll follow me . . .'

He led the way from the hall down a passage and through a baize-covered door to what was clearly the domestic quarters of the house, judging by the more modest furnishing. Halting before another door, he announced over his shoulder, 'This is the housekeeper's room. It's been allocated to me for the time being. No one will disturb us without my permission.'

We entered a comfortable, homely sitting room furnished with a sofa and two armchairs towards which Bardle extended an inviting hand.

'Take a seat, gentlemen,' he said, adding as we sat down, 'what brings you here, Mr Holmes?'

'This,' Holmes replied, reaching into his pocket and producing the copy of the *Lewes Gazette*, folded down to the page where the column under the headline 'LATEST NEWS' was located. Inspector Bardle read it quickly before returning the newspaper to Holmes.

'Aha!' he said with an air of satisfaction. 'So that's why you happen to call in here today. I asked myself what made you turn up like this out of the blue. Now I wonder how you managed to get past those officers I had posted at the entrance to the driveway to send away any visitors.'

It was said in a good-humoured manner, with a touch of self-denigration, as if he were deliberately assuming the role of a not over-bright local bobby and immediately I began to warm to the man. There was a great deal more to Inspector Bardle than met the eye.

Holmes replied in a similar good-natured, dismissive manner.

'Oh that, Inspector! We decided to take the country route through the fields.'

Bardle was not to be outdone.

'Ah, over the stile!' he twinkled back. 'I'll have to make sure there's a constable on duty there as well from now on. Now what can I do for you, Mr Holmes?'

'I called to ask how far you have got with the case,' Holmes replied.

'Not far enough,' Bardle admitted with a rueful shake of his head.

'If there is anything I can do . . .'

Holmes made the suggestion in an offhand manner but Bardle accepted the offer with a sudden and unexpected eagerness, brightening up as if Holmes had lit the man's touch paper and set him aglow.

'Would you be willing, Mr Holmes? I'd be grateful for a helping hand. The trouble is there are so few clues to go on. But let me show you the scene. I'm sure Sir Oliver wouldn't mind. There's only Simmons, the butler, in charge but he's no problem in spite of that lah-di-dah look of his. So come with me and I'll show you what I'm up against.'

Getting to his feet, he set off again for the main hall, Holmes and I at his heels as he climbed the staircase to the upper landing, giving a perfunctory nod to the constable still on guard at its foot. Having reached the top, he turned right and flung open a door leading into a large gallery-like room, lined with glass-fronted showcases, the doors of some of which had been forced open.

'There you are, Mr Holmes!' Bardle announced, waving away a couple of plain-clothed detectives who were dusting one of the cabinet doors with grey powder. 'The Melchett collection and the scene of the crime. Make of it what you will for I admit I'm flummoxed.'

Holmes' attitude seemed to be the very antithesis of Inspector Bardle's. Very calmly and quietly, he crossed the room to examine the cabinet which seemed to contain table silver; along the shelves were displayed salvers and tureens in the precious metal with gaps here and there in the rows of exhibits, indicating where certain pieces were missing. I noticed that throughout his inspection he was careful to touch nothing, keeping his hands clasped behind his back.

'Interesting!' he murmured half to himself, a comment that Bardle quickly took up.

'So what do you make of it, Mr Holmes?' he asked.

'Not a great deal at this early stage,' Holmes admitted, 'except whoever broke into this cabinet had no skill at picking locks. This door has obviously been forced open with a chisel or a strong knife, which implies . . .'

'An amateur?' Bardle suggested.

'That is my conclusion,' Holmes agreed.

'And someone who only wanted the small stuff – the cutlery and the little dishes. He's left behind the bigger pieces like those serving platters or the large pots for serving soup.'

'The tureens,' Holmes interposed. 'Excellent observation, Inspector!'

His tone of voice expressed genuine admiration for Bardle's qualities as a detective at which the man positively glowed, his heavy features normally impassive breaking into a broad smile.

'And also someone who was wearing gloves, judging by the absence of fingerprints on the glass,' Holmes continued.

It was Bardle's turn to be impressed.

'Ah, Mr Holmes!' he remarked, his smile widening still further. 'I wondered if you'd notice that. Now come with me and I'll show you something worth seeing. We'll use the back stairs this time.'

Turning on his heel, he escorted us back to the landing to a second set of stairs, like the hall separated from the main building by a baize-covered door and carpeted with drugget, clearly the servants' access to the upper rooms. Inspector Bardle lead the way, his solid shoulders brushing the walls of the narrow stairway. With his back turned towards us, I risked a question that I had been eager to ask Holmes ever since his scrutiny of the ransacked cabinet.

'Fingerprints?' I hissed.

'Later,' he hissed back.

There was no opportunity to inquire further for we had reached the foot of the stairs and Inspector Bardle, with an unexpected turn of speed, was striding ahead of us through a large kitchen and into an adjoining scullery, the window of which was set open.

'There!' he said triumphantly indicating the

window with a jerk of his thumb. 'There's the way our burglar got in. What do you make of that, Mr Holmes?'

Holmes gave a chuckle.

'Well, whoever he is, he's very small,' he replied.

'A child perhaps?' Inspector Bardle suggested, a reply that took me by surprise.

'A child?' I repeated, quite shocked by the idea. I thought that the employment of young thieves, like that of chimney sweeps, had disappeared years before.

It was the Inspector who responded.

'It's not unheard of, Dr Watson. I myself have had cases where the burglars used children to break into a home. Not being fully grown, they can wriggle their way in through the smallest opening, a fanlight, for example, or in this instance a scullery window. And then once inside, the little villain opens the back door to let in the thief or thieves. I'm sure that's what happened here. I questioned Simmons, the butler, and he admitted that, although the back door was locked, the key was often left in the door and both of the bolts had been drawn when Mrs Davies, the housekeeper, came downstairs to the kitchen early this morning, to put the kettle on.'

'I think that is a very plausible theory,' Holmes agreed although I noticed that, as he spoke, he passed a hand over his chin, a gesture that he often made when he was uncertain of the facts of a case. Inspector Bardle had failed to note this for he was hurrying on with his own account, eager to finish.

'And there's more to come, Mr Holmes. The little scamp, whoever he is, can't have been that well-trained 'cos he left his dabs on the scullery window.'

'Did he indeed!' Holmes exclaimed, sounding quite positive this time. 'What prints are they?'

'A thumb and an index finger.'

'You will let me have them?'

'Of course, Mr Holmes. I'll get Morrison to send copies of them to you.'

'Splendid!' Holmes exclaimed with genuine delight, a mood that lasted when, having taken leave of Inspector Bardle, we set off down the drive, this time by the more conventional route via the main gate, escorted by a uniformed constable who, under Bardle's instructions, was to account for our unexpected appearance to the police on guard, should any explanation be called for.

Holmes, still jubilant, went striding ahead in a manner that indicated he would prefer to postpone any discussion until later, for it was not until we reached The Wheatsheaf a little further down the road and had ensconced ourselves at the table he had booked for us earlier that morning that he referred to our snatched conversation on the back stairs of Melchett Manor.

'You asked about fingerprints. What exactly do you want to know about them, my dear fellow?'

'Well, you have already told me quite a lot, Holmes, how you found them an improvement on the Bertillon method of identification . . .'

'Oh, that system,' Holmes replied dismissively. 'That is quite *passé* as the French might say, even though it was a Frenchman, Alphonse Bertillon, who devised it in the first place. Its disadvantage was you had first to catch your suspect before you could take all those measurements – his height, the size of his feet and his head, not to mention cataloguing the colour of his eyes and hair and then all that had to be classified and filed. It was excessively complicated. Compared to that, fingerprints are so much more straightforward.'

'And so the fingerprints on the scullery window could be vital evidence?'

'Exactly so, Watson.'

'A child's?' I persisted, thinking of Inspector Bardle's comment on the likelihood that whoever had entered the house had childlike proportions.

But Holmes seemed unconvinced by this theory.

'There are other interpretations,' was all he said in reply.

It was one of his deliberately obtuse responses that sometimes used to tease me or, on occasions, to draw me off the scent so that his own interpretation should appear to be even more impressive once the final solution had been established and his theory vindicated. I therefore decided to let the matter rest, although I could not help turning over in my mind possible answers to his remark. Other interpretations? What on earth was he referring to? A dwarf, perhaps? It seemed highly unlikely and yet I supposed it should not be entirely dismissed as a feasible explanation.

He made no further reference to the subject over luncheon and our conversation turned, if I remember correctly, to Elizabethan drama and Shakespeare's sonnets, in particular to the name of the Dark Lady about whom I knew nothing but with which Holmes seemed particularly fascinated, perhaps because of her likeness to our own Dark Lady.

The meal over, we left The Wheatsheaf and returned to the car to drive back, I assumed to Fulworth although, on Holmes' directions, I took a different road to the one we had followed to Lower Melchett. It was a less direct route and it lacked the picturesque features of our morning's drive but Holmes insisted and I followed his instructions. After about half an hour, he said abruptly, 'Stop here!'

We had arrived at the outskirts of an unprepossessing village consisting of a row of brick cottages, one little shop and a tin chapel, the last of which seemed to be Holmes' desired destination, much to my surprise. What could he possibly want there?

But it was apparently not the chapel he was interested in after all; it was another building opposite and in my opinion, equally as unlikely. It was a garage, like the chapel, also constructed of corrugated iron but boasting one dirty window filled with a conglomeration of spare parts for motor cars: tyres, batteries, headlamps, number plates, exhaust pipes, all heaped together higgledy-piggledy.

Without a word of explanation, Holmes disappeared inside the place to emerge about twenty minutes later with a bulky parcel, badly wrapped in brown paper, which he deposited in the back seat of the car, giving me a sideways grin as if to say: 'Go on, Watson. Ask what is in it.'

But I refused to make any response, not even a raised eyebrow. In return, he merely shrugged, accepting my non-compliance with good humour. He played the same little game later in Lewes where he made me halt again while he made a swift foray inside a gentleman's outfitters, returning to the car with yet another parcel, more neatly wrapped this time, which he added to the other package on the back seat.

Again, I made no reference to his actions and as before I received no response from him and we set off for Fulworth, exchanging general pleasantries about our excursion: the beauty of the countryside, the elegance of Melchett Manor and Holmes' particular gratification in renewing his acquaintanceship with Inspector Bardle. However, I noticed nothing was said in reference to the theft of the silver or to the contents of the two parcels, which Holmes whisked away to his bedroom as soon as we arrived at the cottage.

CHAPTER SEVEN

The mystery of the two parcels was solved, at least partially, the following day when over breakfast, Holmes suddenly asked, 'You are not very good at imitating accents, are you Watson?'

'I don't think so, Holmes,' I replied, wondering where this conversation was leading.

'Ah, I thought not,' Holmes said. 'In that case, I shall have to play the main part myself. I'll use my American voice I think.'

'Main part in what?' I asked, much bemused.

'In getting access to Fulworth Hall, of course. We shall have to achieve it somehow, if we're to get the fingerprint proof I need in the Lady in Black case.'

'So you think the theft of the silver from Melchett Manor is connected with that inquiry?'

'All my instincts tell me that is so,' was all he said, but in so positive a tone that I could not dispute it. 'There are too many pieces of evidence that point in that direction.'

'Are there? Such as what?' I asked, not entirely convinced.

'The shapes in the dust we found in the crypt, for one thing.'

'But what significance can they possibly have?'

'They suggested to me that certain objects had been left in there.'

I still failed to follow his reasoning.

'What sort of objects?'

'Fairly heavy ones, for they were clearly impressed into the dust, with bases about five inches square. What objects might fit such dimensions? Oh come, Watson!' he chided me as I failed to come up with an answer. 'Think, my dear fellow!'

'I have no idea,' I admitted, totally at a loss.

'Candlesticks?' he suggested. 'Heavy ones that would stand on a sideboard or dining room table. I must admit that at the time I also noticed spots of candle wax on the floor, which I did not mention. You know me, Watson. I have a tendency to be secretive at times just to tease you. However, I did show you that other piece of evidence, that little object I found on the steps leading down to the crypt. It was that which confirmed my suspicions.'

'The little metal object that looked as if someone had trodden on it? What was it?'

'This you mean?' he asked, reaching into his pocket and showing it to me on the palm of his hand. But I was as bewildered by it as the first time Holmes had shown it to me.

'It is a little silver spoon,' Holmes continued, 'of the type you would find in a salt dish as part of a condiment set, again found on a dinner table.'

'Oh, I see!' I exclaimed. 'So you think there's a connection with the silverware that was stolen from Melchett Manor?'

'Yes, I do.'

'And that the Lady in Black is also connected with it?'

'Yes, again, although I'm still not quite certain where she fits in. That's why I need to find out whose fingerprints are on the pantry window.'

'But how do you propose doing that?'

'I'll show you,' Holmes replied.

Going over to the desk that stood in one of the fireplace alcoves, he took out a small cardboard box, which he opened. Inside were about a dozen visiting cards, which he had collected when we were still living in Baker Street, and which he had specially printed as useful proof of the various identities he assumed at times during his career as a private consulting detective. From the box, he carefully extracted a card, holding it by one corner as he laid it down on the table, saying sharply to me as he did so, 'Don't pick it up, Watson; you may ruin my whole plan.'

It was an ordinary looking visiting card on which was printed: *William K. Goldstein, Book Dealer, 901 Parkway Avenue, Boston, USA*. Below this was added: *Top Prices Guaranteed.*

'So what part is he supposed to play in your "plan", Holmes?' I asked.

'With a little luck, he will introduce me to the occupant of Fulworth Hall, our Lady in Black, whose fingerprints Inspector Bardle will identify with those found in Melchett Manor.'

'Oh, I see,' I replied, feeling a little let down that Holmes had not confided all this to me at the beginning.

Holmes, aware of my reaction, hastily made amends.

'I confess I haven't been completely frank with you, my dear fellow, for which I sincerely apologise. As I have said to you before, I need your assistance with certain problems. You help me to think them through. That is why I invited you to visit me, a situation of which I think you are aware. But that does not mean I underrate your company in any way. I value most highly your honesty and your loyalty. I could not wish for a better friend in the world.'

I was so taken aback by Holmes' remarks that I could not make any reply and even after I had cleared my throat, my voice sounded hoarse and unreal.

'Thank you, Holmes,' I mumbled, at which he laughed and, slapping me on the shoulder, said, 'Come, let us get down to business – the Lady in Black mystery and its solution.

'You see, my old friend, I had so few facts to go on. She was a woman, she wore black, so she was possibly a widow, she was in her mid-forties; she had a manservant who apparently took care of her; she probably lived in Fulworth Hall; the beach and the sea in Fulworth Cove evidently had some special significance to her. That was all.

'I tried to find out more about her from other people in the village but there was not much they could tell me either. Nobody ever saw her, although they thought she had moved into Fulworth Hall about nine years ago. As for the manservant, he was almost as inconspicuous as his mistress although I managed to collect up a few details: he drove a van, he apparently did the shopping, but never in the village, usually in Lewes but where else no one knew for certain. No letters were delivered at the Hall, not even a newspaper and no one ever visited the house. The local people, even Mrs B, did not know their names or where they came from. I even asked the estate agent in Lewes who had handled the letting of the house but he couldn't tell me much either. The man called there every Michaelmas day to pay for the lease in cash and that was all.'

'Surely there were papers to do with the leasehold that someone must have signed?' I asked, finding myself as curious as Holmes over the situation.

He gave a little ironic laugh.

'Yes, there were; signed by John Smith, of course, but nothing more.'

'So what are you going to do, Holmes? I imagine Mr Smith has something to do with it?'

'Good reasoning, my dear fellow. He must indeed. You and I will call at Fulworth Hall, you as my driver, myself as William K. Goldstein; an American bibliophile who has heard that a cache of books and printed papers regarding early Victorian novelists has been found at the Hall and that the owners are willing to sell. As a collector of such literary material, I am eager to buy. So I have come to England especially to arrange a deal. To confirm my identity, I shall hand the card to anyone who answers the door, hoping . . .'

Here he paused and raised an eyebrow.

'That whoever takes it will leave their fingerprints on it?' I suggested.

'Oh, well done, Watson! We'll make a private detective consultant of you yet.'

'What happens after that?' I asked.

'I shall ask Inspector Bardle to compare the prints

on the card with those found on the scullery window at Melchett Manor and with a little luck, we shall find a match.'

'And if there isn't?' I asked.

'Oh, don't throw cold water on the plan yet!' he protested. 'Let us hope Lady Luck is on our side in the matter.'

'And whatever is in the parcels is part of the plan?' I continued.

'If you wait a moment, I'll show you,' he said and left the room to go upstairs where I heard him rummaging around in his bedroom, returning shortly afterwards with the two brown paper packages, which he opened and laid down on the table. In addition, there was a third packet, much smaller than the others, containing a pair of side whiskers for Holmes and a small moustache for me which I suspected had come from Holmes' original Baker Street collection of disguises.

The contents of the other two parcels were a strange mixture of objects. In the badly wrapped parcel, which he had collected from the little shop selling motor vehicle parts, were two pairs of licence plates and a few screws wrapped up in a twist of newspaper; the second, the one from the gentlemen's outfit in Lewes, contained a green uniform jacket, such as a chauffeur might wear, and a matching peaked cap which Holmes set down on my head.

'It fits!' he exclaimed. 'I hoped it would but I had to guess the size. I didn't want to give the game away by asking you.'

'So what exactly is the game?' I asked. 'I assume I dress up as a chauffeur and drive you up to Fulworth Hall. But I am a little bewildered by the licence plates. Do I carry them? Or wear them around my neck?'

We both burst out laughing at this point, the sort of laughter that clears the air and confirms a relationship between two people.

'No, my dear Watson,' Holmes explained when we had both recovered, 'we screw them on the car in place of the original plates so that, if someone notices them, they can't be traced.'

'You mean *I* shall screw them on,' I corrected him, never having seen Holmes handle a screwdriver in my long acquaintance with him.

'Well, if you insist,' he flashed back. 'But let's start for heaven's sake. Mrs B will be arriving soon and what she will make of the pair of us defeats imagination, at least mine.'

In the event, I found the screws were not needed, after all, having discovered the original connections were so firmly fixed that they were immovable and I had to fasten the number plates on with wire. That done, we changed our outfits to suit our new identities, myself in the green jacket, cap and wearing the moustache, Holmes in the side whiskers, cape and deer stalker, which he thought would live up to his image of an American bibliophile in England in search of Victorian literature.

As Fulworth Hall was not far away, it took merely a few minutes to drive there, only to find the gate to the driveway was firmly padlocked and we were reduced to abandoning the car and squeezing around the end of one of the gateposts to make our entrance; not a very dignified way of arriving and I hoped no one in the house had witnessed it.

But, as we crunched our way up the drive over the gravel, there seemed no one about: no curtain twitched, no face appeared at the window, the place appeared to be deserted.

In my role, as a hired chauffeur, I thought it best to remain at the foot of the steps, letting Holmes mount them alone, carrying, I noticed, the visiting card, which he carefully held by one corner. While I waited, I took a quick glance about me, taking in the details of Fulworth Hall and its setting for the sake of my own curiosity.

It must have been an imposing place at one time, I imagined, with its portico and tiers of windows. But all it presented now was a travesty of its former beauty. Large pieces of stucco had fallen from the walls and pillars, revealing the bare brick that lay behind, while the paint had shrivelled off the wooden frames of the windows like scabs.

As for the garden, that, too, had suffered the same neglect. There had once been a large lawn in front of the house, edged with flower borders and ornamental shrubs. All that remained was an oblong of shaggy grass and strips of unkempt ground dense with weeds and brambles.

The rest of the garden was no better. Overgrown trees and bushes crowded out the view apart from a few glimpses of the cliffs and the far-off glitter of the sea. The only access to the cove was a dilapidated picket gate, that hung on its hinges, which I assumed led to the flight of steps down to the beach.

Holmes meanwhile had knocked on the door with the round iron that hung in its centre and, receiving no reply, had knocked again.

This time someone answered. At least, the door was opened a grudging few inches and a man's face appeared at the gap.

'Mr Whittaker?' Holmes asked, speaking with the same American accent that he was to use later in August 1914 just before the outbreak of the Great War in bringing about the arrest of Von Bork, head of a German espionage ring that was sending vital information to the Kaiser about the British navy, such as the movement of shipping and other naval secrets, crucial to our success in the coming conflict.

Before the man had a chance to reply, Holmes had thrust the visiting card through the narrow opening in such a brisk, positive manner that the man had to take it. But not for long. A second later he had pushed it back at Holmes who had begun his little introductory speech he had practised over breakfast, about Victorian novels, and how he had been told that Mr and Mrs Whittaker of Fulwell Hall might be willing to sell and oh, how excited he was at the chance.

It was at that point that the man opened the door a little further in order to give himself room to return the card, saying abruptly as he did so, 'You've come to the wrong address. This isn't Fulwell Hall,' before slamming the door shut.

The encounter lasted only a few seconds, just long enough for me to catch a glimpse of the man's features – an elderly man in his mid to late seventies, I estimated; almost bald but with wisps of grey hair still clinging to his scalp; skin wrinkled and leathery as if from long exposure to the sun and wind; voice, hoarse and with an accent I could not quite locate except it sounded northern – Manchester, perhaps? Or Birmingham?

As for the interior of the house, I caught no sight of that at all before the door shut.

Holmes came down the steps towards me, shrugging his shoulders and grimacing, as if he was not entirely sure if the little gambit had been successful or not, but he was holding the visiting card tenderly by one corner and he wiggled it at me as if to signify he was hoping for the best.

Conscious that we might still be under observation by the man who had answered the door, we continued to maintain our roles, Holmes going ahead and getting into the back seat of the car having squeezed himself round the gate, I following a few steps behind before climbing in behind the wheel and starting the engine. Neither of us spoke until we were a good few yards from Fulworth Hall and safely out of sight around a corner in the road.

'Well, did it work?' I asked, impatient to find out Holmes' real impressions of his success or failure.

However, he still remained doubtful.

'I still can't decide,' he replied. 'The man took the card as I had hoped so his prints should be on it. But I have my doubts he was the person who climbed in through that window. If I am right, then the whole affair is a waste of time.'

He sounded so downcast that I hastened to cheer him up.

'If he wasn't the man, then there might be other prints that Inspector Bardle found at Melchett Manor, perhaps on the cabinet that was broken into that will match up?' I suggested.

'Perhaps,' he agreed but not very positively. 'We must wait for Bardle's confirmation on that.'

As he spoke, he was carefully stowing away the

visiting card into a special pocketbook he had carried with him, which I remembered from our Baker Street days for the safe keeping of such pieces of evidence.

'So what do we do now?' I asked. 'We can hardly go back to the cottage. Mrs B will be there. She'll surely notice our disguises. You know what she is like.'

'Only too well,' he agreed, taking off the deerstalker hat and throwing it onto the back seat of the car, remarking contemptuously as he did so, 'Ridiculous headgear! I've never liked it!'

'Shall we go to the Fisherman's Arms then?' I suggested.

'Not there either; Reg Berry and his wife will notice us, and while they're not as inquisitive as Mrs B, they might still be a little too curious. Drive into Lewes, Watson. We'll find somewhere there.'

In the end, we found refuge in a prim little café in a side street where we drank tea and tried not to look too conspicuous but even stripped of our caps, false moustaches and such like accoutrements we still drew the attention of the other customers, consisting entirely of elderly ladies, and were glad to creep away when at last the time came when Mrs B would have left the cottage and it was safe for us to go home.

As Holmes remarked gratefully as we drew up by the front of his beehives, 'Thank heavens that's over. We can only hope Inspector Bardle's report is satisfactory and we don't have to go through another ridiculous ruse like that again.'

'And Langdale Pike's report,' I reminded him.

'His, too,' Holmes replied. 'In fact I think his is possibly the most important.'

CHAPTER EIGHT

There was no mystery attached to Holmes' mood during the next few days. With increasing impatience, he waited for Langdale Pike's answer to his request for information regarding the Trevalyan family and for Inspector Bardle to contact him about the fingerprints found on the scullery window at Melchett Manor, although the latter seemed of lesser importance. It was Langdale Pike's delay that caused my old friend the greatest discomfort.

Every morning, at the time when the first post was due to arrive, he paced up and down the living room waiting for the rattle of the letterbox that heralded the delivery of the mail. As soon as he heard it, he raced into the hall, abandoning his breakfast, to return empty-handed apart from a clutch of unwanted correspondence, which he threw down on the table in disgust.

So anxious was he not to miss the delivery that he was even unwilling to leave the house and it was only the expected arrival of Mrs B that drove him out. Even so, we never went far, only to the cove where he had seen the Lady in Black and where he prowled up and down the beach or seated himself on the rock where she had sat and like her, gazed out to sea.

This state of mind continued for several days and I was also beginning to find the situation distressing, not for my own sake, although Holmes was not his usual companionable self, but for the return of certain patterns of behaviour that had occurred during his old Baker Street days and I was concerned that he might revert to some of his earlier habits, in short, his use of cocaine.

I was therefore immensely relieved when, on the morning of the fourth day, the letterbox gave its customary rattle and he rose from the table to answer its summons, rather reluctantly, I thought as if not expecting any positive news, when I heard him give a delighted exclamation. Moments later he returned from the hall waving an envelope above his head like a victory flag.

'It has come at last!' he cried and with no further ado, he flung himself down on his chair and, in his eagerness, slit the envelope open with the butter knife before extracting several sheets of paper which he immediately began to read, totally engrossed in their contents.

I knew better than to interrupt his concentration although, judging from his responses, he was not wholly satisfied with Langdale Pike's report and it crossed my mind that if Holmes had a telephone installed in his cottage, it would make contact with people such as Langdale Pike much simpler. It would certainly make it easier for me to speak to my wife. As matters stood, I would have to go to the post office in the village in order to let her know when to expect me to return home. It was obvious that my stay in Fulworth was likely to be longer than Holmes' invitation to a week's holiday with him in Sussex.

'Good news?' I asked when Holmes laid aside Langdale Pike's report.

'Yes, on the whole,' he replied. 'Pike has evidently gone to some length to cover most of the information I asked for.'

'Such as?' I prompted, eager to know all the details.

But he refused to be tempted. Rising to his feet, he thrust the letter into his pocket, announcing as he did so, 'It is too complex to discuss now. Besides Mrs B will arrive at any moment. So I suggest we go somewhere quiet where we can talk in complete privacy.'

The 'somewhere' he referred to was, as I had expected, the cove, the most appropriate setting for any conversation that concerned the Lady in Black, so I was not surprised when, after we had descended the steps, we set off across the beach to the rock where Holmes had first seen her sitting and gazing out towards the sea.

'Now,' he said retrieving the letter from his pocket, 'let us first deal with the Trevalyan connection. Langdale Pike has gone to the trouble of drawing up a genealogical history, interesting but not relevant apart from the more recent family members, in particular Henry Trevalyan whose rather grand tomb is, as we know, in the vault at St Botolph's and who, according to Mrs B, and confirmed by Langdale Pike, died in 1870 at the age of seventy-five, leaving behind a widow and a daughter. As Mrs B also informed us, they had only one child, Henrietta, no doubt named after her father. She was usually known as Hetty and she ran away from school to elope with a man she had met in Lewes. As a result she was disinherited by her father. All this information is confirmed by Langdale Pike.

'It was at this point that Mrs B's information ran out, but thanks to Pike's enquiries, we can now follow up the details of Hetty's later life.

'The man she eloped with was George Sutton, a well-to-do, forty-year-old bachelor from

Birmingham who owned a successful building firm.'

'Forty years old!' I exclaimed. 'Why, he was old enough to be her father!'

'Exactly, Watson. You have, as they say, hit the nail on the head. In my opinion, I think Hetty may have chosen him as a surrogate father, someone kind and considerate, unlike her own father. And George Sutton may have chosen her as a substitute daughter. One can understand Henry Trevalyan's reaction to his daughter's marriage; not only to a man old enough to be a father but to a *builder* for goodness' sake: a tradesman in other words, whereas he was trying to create a lord-of-the-manor image for himself. It was much too demeaning for him to accept.'

Here Holmes paused and raising a quizzical eyebrow in my direction, asked, 'Does anything about this account strike you as significant, Watson?'

Not sure what he was referring to, I replied, 'Significant, Holmes? No, not really.'

'That is because you are a man, my dear fellow, like Langdale Pike. You are seeing the situation entirely from a man's point of view. No one has given a thought to what effect all this had on Mrs Trevalyan and her family. After all, Hetty was as much her daughter as Henry Trevalyan's, as well as her mother's granddaughter. They, too, may have been as displeased as Henry Trevalyan by Hetty's marriage to a man twenty-three years her senior, even though he was a wealthy businessman.'

'I see what you mean, Holmes. Does Langdale Pike refer to them?'

'No, not at all. That is my point. As a man, he is concerned only with the male side of the family. We can, of course, follow up the female side ourselves if need be. I often think,' he added in a musing tone, 'that even our language has the same gender bias embedded in it. Take, for example, the word "history". Why not *her*story? The 'his' part of it comes from the Greek word, "history", meaning "a wise man". The Anglo-Saxons were no better. The very word "woman" derives from their term "wifman". Mark my words, Watson, one of these days the women will rise up and demand their rights to equality and heaven alone knows what will come of it. Lady judges? Female bishops? Women in Parliament? Perhaps even a "wifman" prime minister? But they'll probably be no worse than their present male counterparts; even better; at least one must hope so.

'But all this is beside the point. To continue with Hetty Trevalyan's story. According to Langdale Pike, she eloped with George Sutton to Birmingham where they married and set up home in one of Sutton's very comfortable, newly built villas, containing every modern convenience a bride could wish for, including not one but two carriages and a bevy of servants.

They soon became part of an affluent group of Birmingham residents, mostly successful businessmen and their wives with whom they enjoyed a very pleasant social life, probably far better than Hetty would have known in Fulworth.

'Some time later, they had a daughter whom they christened Eleanor, possibly after the child's maternal grandmother although unfortunately Pike does not comment on this aspect of the family tree. When the child was five, her father suddenly died of a heart attack, a great shock to his widow who was grief-stricken and for a time became a virtual recluse. Do you have any comment to make on this, Watson?'

He was regarding me with bright-eyed attention and, a little bemused, I shook my head.

'Oh, come, come!' he admonished me. 'You disappoint me; I thought you would have had more sensitivity. You are a doctor so you must have had to deal with the death of certain of your patients during your career and witness the grief of those who were close to them. What do you do in such circumstances?'

I was deeply disturbed by Holmes' comments. Of course I was aware of the effects such tragedies had on their loved ones. In fact, I had experienced a great personal loss myself when my first wife died and, despite the happiness that my second marriage had brought me and my gratitude for that consolation, I was still aware of a sense of bereavement that time had not fully healed.

I also remembered my own distress when, years earlier, I had stood on the edge of Reichenbach Falls in the Swiss Alps, convinced that Holmes had plunged to his death with Moriarty, his arch-enemy, as they grappled together on the edge of the ravine.

So Holmes' remarks, which I took to be a criticism of my lack of sensitivity, cut me to the quick. It seemed so unjust. While I had mourned his loss, how had he responded? He had lain hidden on a ledge above the falls, observing what happened with an objective eye, untouched, it seemed, by any emotion.

And yet, this dispassionate attitude was one of his greatest assets, I suddenly realised. Unlike myself, or Langdale Pike, or Henry Trevalyan, or any other man who was involved in the Lady in Black inquiry only Holmes alone could successfully interpret the plot and the actors who took part in it. I also realised that when in the past I had described him as being cold-blooded and lacking in feeling, I had seriously misjudged him. Yes, he had indeed little sentiment, but that was his nature, and I had either to accept it or reject it and the latter option was quite out of the question. So, although it was a bitter pill to swallow, I gave way and admitted my inability to understand with a gesture of acceptance.

Holmes, who had been regarding me with that

intense gaze of his, now softened his expression and, leaning forward, touched me briefly on the shoulder, remarking as he did so, 'You see, my dear Watson, we both have to transfer our line of inquiry from the men to the women in the case, to Hetty and her family connections and also to her daughter. They must from now on take centre stage. According to Langdale Pike, Hetty was deeply affected by her husband's death, for a time at least, becoming something of a recluse.

'However, he said nothing about the daughter who was five years old when her father died. How did she respond? Or, come to that her grandparents, the Suttons, on her father's side? In fact, Langdale Pike fails to mention them at all. So we know nothing about their relationship with one another. Did Hetty visit them? Or did they visit Hetty? What was their reaction to George Sutton's death or Henry Trevalyan disinheriting their daughter-in-law? There are so many questions that remain unanswered.'

'So what do you propose doing about it, Holmes?'

'I suppose I shall have to write to Pike again, although I am reluctant to do so. He takes so long to reply. The waiting plays havoc with my nervous system.'

And with mine too, I added silently.

Out loud, I said, 'If you had a telephone installed here, you could speak directly to Langdale Pike, instead of having to wait for him to write to you. Wouldn't that be easier?'

Holmes regarded me with a long, direct gaze before replying, 'I dislike telephones, Watson,' he said dismissively.

'But you had one in Baker Street,' I pointed out.

'That was London, my dear fellow. This is Sussex, quite a different kettle of fish. I would rather not have the peace of the countryside shattered by the ringing of one of those wretched instruments. However, I see your point. A telephone would speed up matters. Perhaps I should submit to the modern way of life, loath though I am to admit defeat. But having one installed will take several days, I should imagine. What shall I do in the meantime?'

'Couldn't Mrs B help? She seems to know quite a lot about the family.'

'Oh for heaven's sake, Watson! In her own way, she is almost as infuriating as Pike!'

He broke off suddenly in the middle of his protestation.

'Wait a moment though! I think you may have the answer!' he exclaimed.

'Have I, Holmes?' I asked, delighted that I might have solved the problem but not sure how I had managed to do it.

'Let me think,' he continued, ignoring me and addressing himself.

Turning abruptly on his heel, he took several short paces up and down the room, slapping his forehead with his open palm as if the rhythm of the repeated blows might release some half-forgotten memory. Then, as suddenly as he had sprung into motion, he stopped and spun back towards me; his face vivid with excitement.

'Of course! I remember now! When Mrs B spoke of the Trevalyans, she mentioned Mrs Trevalyan's family. Can you recall what she said?'

'Yes, at least some of it,' I replied hesitantly, unable to summon up any clear recollection of the occasion but anxious to appease Holmes for whom the information was evidently crucial. 'She said something about them being a farming family who had lived in the same village for generations . . .'

'Never mind all that! Their name, Watson! That is what I want. It was something similar to Lackham, was it not? Or Laycock?'

The name suddenly popped into my mind without any effort on my part and to my great surprise, I heard myself enunciating it.

'The Lockharts, Holmes!' I cried out.

'Of course! Of course!' he exclaimed, crossing the room to thump me on the back. 'The Lockharts of Barton! Well done, Watson! What a genius you are!'

I felt hugely gratified by his compliments but a little guilty as well, as I had contributed so little to deserve it. But there was no opportunity to do anything about it for Holmes was on the move again, bustling over to the door and urging me to be quick.

'Get your coat on, Watson and make sure you have the car keys!'

'Where are we going?' I asked, bewildered by this sudden turn of events.

'To Barton, of course,' he retorted, as if I should have known that all along. 'Come on! Hurry up! Mrs B will be here at any moment and she will keep us here for hours.'

The remark was something of an exaggeration but I took his point and, having gathered up my keys, my coat and my stick, I followed him out of the door to the car, feeling harassed.

My sense of inadequacy was suddenly changed to one of exasperation. Much to my dismay, Holmes seemed to have reverted to his old idiosyncratic behaviour of his Baker Street days, selfish and demanding, which at times had strained our relationship almost to breaking point.

Turning on the engine, I asked, keeping my voice as level as possible, 'I know we are going to Barton, Holmes. But where *exactly* is Barton and which road should I take?'

There was a silence in which I wondered if I had exacerbated the situation when to my relief, I hear him laugh and, when I turned my head, I saw he was observing me with a very apologetic grin.

'I am not sure myself,' he admitted, 'but it is somewhere off the road to Lower Melchett we took the other day. So go to Fulworth, take the Melchett road and, after that, we shall have to follow the signposts.'

Smiling back at him, I put the car into gear and drove up the lane, turning to the left at the top of the hill on to the Fulworth road. Halfway down, I caught a glimpse of Mrs B on her way up to the cottage, I assumed, bending low over her bicycle as she toiled up the slope. She was wearing her hat with the bunch of cotton violets decorating the brim, her house shoes and her overall stuffed into the basket on the front of the handlebars.

I was about to raise a hand in greeting but as Holmes made a hasty gesture of dismissal, I refrained from acknowledging her presence and so we passed each other on the road as if we were strangers.

Having arrived at Fulworth, it was easy to follow the signposts, first down the familiar route to Lower Melchett and then, at a crossroads, to take a turning to the left to Barton, about five miles to the north.

Like Lower Melchett, it was some distance from the sea and situated in a similar landscape of gently rolling meadows and pastures. Slightly larger than the other village, it boasted a small high street comprising a butcher's, a grocer's and a newsagent's cum post office. There was also a school, a two-gabled, red-brick building with a wooden belfry for summoning the local children to their classrooms, two public houses, the Crown and the Red Lion, and a church with a tower that had its own belfry, as well as a large churchyard stretching out behind a flint wall.

It was here that Holmes told me to stop and I pulled over to the verge near a gate leading on to a gravelled path that in turn led to the church. Before I had a chance to switch off the engine, Holmes had climbed out of the passenger seat and was striding purposefully down the path to the church porch where he stood waiting impatiently for me to catch up with him.

'Now Watson,' he said when at last I joined him, 'I suggest we divide the churchyard into two sections, you take the right-hand side while I take the left.' He stopped at this point to look sharply at me. 'You know what we are looking for?'

I could easily have pleaded ignorance or given some facetious reply such as 'a pot of gold' but good sense got the better of me.

'The Lockharts' grave?' I suggested, keeping my face straight.

'Exactly,' he agreed. 'Now let us make a start. Call me if you find it.'

In any event, it was Holmes who made the

discovery, which he announced with a triumphant 'Halloo!' such as signals the sighting of a fox in a hunt, and waved his arms to beckon me to join him.

Unlike the graveyard at St Botolph's, this one, St Michael's as we found out later, was well maintained, the grass between the graves cut close and the graves themselves planted with flowers or rose bushes or, in some instances, covered with a layer of glittering coloured stones, like outsize bath crystals, that seemed out of keeping with the more sober style of the rest of the memorials.

The Lockharts' grave displayed the more muted attitude to death. It was marked by a plain white marble cross on the base of which rested a book, also of white marble, open at a double page, on the left-hand leaf of which was inscribed a column of names, while adjacent on the right-hand side were the dates of the births and deaths of each individual, under the general heading *IN LOVING MEMORY*. Seeing it, I could not help comparing this simple family tombstone with the large, ostentatious sarcophagus dedicated solely to Henry Trevalyan that dominated the crypt of St Botolph's.

Holmes, who had produced a notebook from his pocket, began to jot down the details of one of the inscriptions that read: *Eleanor Trevalyan, born 17th April 1827 – died 4th November 1879.*

'So we now know Mrs Trevalyan's full name and

Mrs B was right when she said she wasn't buried with her husband . . .' I began but before I could complete the sentence, Holmes silenced me with a quick thrust of his elbow into my ribs and a nod of his head to the right.

Following his gaze, I saw a short, self-important looking figure standing at the foot of the grave and watching us with bright-eyed attention. His curiosity reminded me of Mrs B's inquisitiveness but while hers had been obvious, his had a more intelligent edge to it. Realising Holmes and I were aware of his presence, he stepped forward holding out a hand in greeting.

'Is there anything I can do to help you, gentleman?' he asked. 'By the way, I'm Lionel Larkin, one of St Michael's churchwardens. Are you by any chance interested in genealogy? If you are, I may be able to assist you. I have made quite a detailed study of some of the local families. It is quite a hobby of mine.'

'Really?' Holmes replied. 'Now that could be most useful, Mr Larkin. As a matter of fact, I am researching into my late grandmother's background who may be related to the Lockharts.'

I knew Holmes was lying shamelessly but it was in a good cause and he kept the same bland expression as he added, 'I should be most grateful if you could tell me where the Lockharts used to live. I have not been able to trace any addresses for them.'

'Oh, that is no problem, Mr . . .'

'Gifford,' Holmes put in. 'James Gifford. And this,' he continued turning to me, 'is an old colleague of mine, Frederick Swayne.'

Goodness knows where he had acquired the name but it came so pat that it seemed it must have been familiar to him. Anyway, there was no opportunity to ask and all I could do was to shake hands with Lionel Larkin who remarked, 'Delighted to meet you, Mr Swayne,' before turning back to Holmes.

'I can certainly give you the Lockharts' address, Mr Gifford. It's Abbot's Farm, along Martin's Lane which is over there to the left past the Red Lion,' pointing a finger. 'You'll see the farm on the right about half a mile down the lane. It's a lovely location. I do hope you can find your antecedents, Mr Gifford,' he continued. 'I have had so much pleasure searching for mine. It can lead to such interesting results. For instance, I discovered that I myself am connected to the Swaffhams of Orpington. In fact, I might have inherited the title and become Sir Lionel Swaffham, if only my father had been a Swaffham. I went especially to Orpington to look at the family house; a beautiful mansion with a lake and a tennis court. To think I could have inherited it all!'

As he was speaking, I felt Holmes stiffen beside me and I wondered what Larkin had said to catch his interest so suddenly. Even Larkin himself, absorbed though he was in his own genealogy, became aware that he had talked for too long and lost Holmes' attention for he broke off to add, 'But I mustn't take up more of your time, Mr Gifford, and yours too, Mr Swayne. It has been such a pleasure meeting you both.'

It was said with such genuine sincerity that I began to feel guilty, that we were cutting him short, a point I made to Holmes as he hustled me out of the churchyard to the car.

'My dear Watson, you are much too patient with the Larkins of this world. If we had not made a move, he would still be chattering on about the Swaffhams. However, to give him his due, he has unwittingly done us a great service by directing us to a new and crucial line of investigation in our inquiries.'

'Has he? What line is that?'

'You will soon find out,' he replied infuriatingly.

We had reached the car and, as we got in, he added, 'Stop at the post office on the way, there's a good fellow. There's a little bit of business I want to do before we go to the farm.'

Whatever the 'little bit of business' involved, it was a good half an hour before Holmes finally emerged, looking very pleased with himself.

'Now to Abbot's Farm,' he said, giving me a sly, sideways glance, 'but not too fast, Swayne. I would like to admire the countryside as we go.'

'Swayne!' I exclaimed, remembering it was the name that Holmes had given me earlier. 'Why Swayne? Who was he?'

'If you must know, he was a very skilful pickpocket who robbed Sir Lionel Swaffham of Orpington of a valuable watch and chain.'

'Oh, Holmes!' I protested. 'Be serious!'

'Then, to be serious, if you insist, I really cannot remember who Swayne is or was. He is obviously someone from my past whom I hope is an honest citizen, worth remembering. Anyway, what does it matter? It shall be your alter ego from now on. What does matter is my decision to have a telephone installed in the cottage.'

'Really?' I was amazed. 'But I thought you disliked them.'

'I still do. But I see your point and I shall accept it. So let us proceed to carrying through the next piece of useful advice that I have been given this morning.'

'Whose advice is that?' I asked as I started the engine.

'Lionel Larkin, of all people.'

I was even more amazed.

'But . . .' I began.

'I know, I know.' Holmes interrupted me tetchily. 'However, one lives and learns, according to that infuriatingly smug axiom. So let us try putting it into practice, shall we?'

He waved a hand towards the road to indicate to drive on.

It was only a short journey down a lane lined with trees and broad grassy verges, overflowing with cow parsley and pink willowherb and those long-stemmed daisies that grow in abundance in the ditches.

As Lionel Larkin had told us, Abbot's Farm lay to the right. It was a large, rambling house, built partly of ancient brick and tile, some of it beamed and plastered, its roof thatched in places, the windows mullioned. It seemed not to have been constructed by human hands but to have grown out of the earth like the trees and the wild flowers that surrounded it.

I drew into the side of the road and switched off the engine and the two of us sat there gazing at it, as if enchanted, the silence broken only by an unseen bird that was singing its heart out somewhere across the road among the sunlit leaves.

After a few moments, Holmes stirred and murmured, 'Ah! I see now what Larkin meant about location.'

'Do you want to go up to the house?' I asked.

'What, and shatter the dream? No, no, Watson. Never. Let it sleep. But you can see now, can you not, my antipathy towards the telephone? Imagine that ringing out, breaking the stillness and silencing the bird. But I realise it has its uses. We must go on following Larkin's advice and find the other location.'

'What other location?' I asked, a little bewildered by his answer.

'The one we have not yet seen,' was his only reply and I had to be satisfied for on the drive back to Fulworth, he made no further reference to it, turning the conversation to a dissertation on Greek philosophy and other topics quite unconnected to the Lady in Black investigation.

CHAPTER NINE

Three days later the engineer arrived to install the telephone and, while we waited, Holmes and I took ourselves off for what was almost the holiday that Holmes had invited me to Fulworth for in the first place. He was in a good mood and we spent the time very pleasantly, walking on the Downs, admiring the countryside and the glimpses of the sea between their gentle grassy slopes, eating luncheon at the Fisherman's Arms, where we were warmly welcomed by the landlord and his regular clients, and, of course, going down to the cove where we sat on the Lady in Black rock, as Holmes had christened it, peering up at Fulworth Hall, or what could be seen of it through the surrounding trees, or watching the waves come creeping in up the beach.

Mrs B had been allowed the day off when the telephone was installed, in order to give the engineer a clear, uninterrupted run and on Holmes' instruction it had been located in his workroom, out of earshot of any eavesdroppers, a choice made with Mrs B in mind, I suspected. As the guest, I was given the honour of baptising the instrument, so to speak, by making the first call to my wife to ensure all was well and to be assured myself that she was in good health and that my locum was managing my practice without any problems.

Holmes made the second call to Harold Stackhurst, whom we had not seen for several days, to inform him he could now be contacted via the telephone, and to give him the number. As I left the room, I heard Holmes exclaim 'Really?' in a surprised tone of voice, as if Stackhurst had said something quite unexpected and when he returned downstairs he still looked astonished.

'Harold Stackhurst has just told me he is getting married!' he announced.

'Married!' I repeated. 'Who to?'

'He didn't say.'

'Perhaps to the mother of one of his students,' I suggested.

'We shall find out on Saturday evening. Stackhurst is giving a party at The Gables to celebrate the betrothal to which we've been invited.'

'You've accepted?' I asked.

'Of course, I would not miss it for the world,' he replied before repeating half to himself, as if still astonished by the news, 'Stackhurst getting married! There must be romance in the air, like a fever. I wonder if anyone else will succumb to the infection.'

'Not Ian Murdoch and Maud Bellamy, I hope,' I protested, thinking of the occasion when Holmes and I had last seen them together, and Murdoch had shown a disturbing inclination, I thought, to control her.

Holmes gave a little shrug.

'There is no point in speculating about it, Watson. Besides, it is none of our business. All I can suggest is we buy a bottle of champagne for the happy couple, flowers for the bride-to-be and assume a pleasant expression on Saturday evening whatever the outcome. I also advise both of us to forget about it in the meantime and concentrate instead on our own more immediate concern, the solution to the Lady in Black inquiry, which reminds me. I must telephone Langdale Pike and give him my number. Oh, what a mixed blessing that wretched instrument is! If I am not careful, people will start ringing me day and night. *Ringing!* What a suitable verb for the dreadful clamour it makes. But whatever happens, Mrs B must not be given the number or she will be *ringing* me from the local post office, wanting a little chat.'

He postponed his call to Langdale Pike until after breakfast, returning from his workroom a little later in a much more jaunty mood.

'At least that is something to rejoice about,' he announced. 'Langdale Pike has completed those inquires I asked him to make. He will be coming here tomorrow afternoon to discuss the case with me.'

'He is coming *here*!' I asked, much surprised by the news. As far as I knew, Langdale Pike rarely left his London club.

'Indeed he is. He has arranged to hire a car and a driver and will arrive here about three o'clock. I think it's his way of repaying the debt he owes me for all the titbits of gossip I gave him for his newspaper column.'

'But how on earth did you manage to persuade him?' I asked.

'By offering him a sweetmeat,' Holmes replied.

'What sort of a sweetmeat?'

'The promise of an exclusive interview with Lady Agatha Crispin-Jones about her trip to Africa to go big-game hunting.'

'And how did you arrange that?'

'By promising *her* the publicity she would acquire through Pike's article on her derring-do when faced with hungry lion.' Giving me one of his self-deprecatory lopsided grins he added, 'I telephoned them both to set up the arrangement.

So I admit it has its uses even though I still dislike it intensely.'

The following day we had a hasty luncheon at the Fisherman's Arms before returning to the cottage in good time for Langdale Pike's arrival.

Not having met him before, I was most curious to make his acquaintance, knowing very little about gossip writers and their way of life, although I gathered from Holmes that Langdale Pike made a very comfortable living at what seemed to me to be a rather dubious profession, hence his ability to afford a hired car and chauffeur.

He was older than I had imagined with silvery-grey hair swept back on each side of his forehead from a centre parting and pale blue eyes that had a steely look to them, despite the languid, rather foppish air suggested by his flowing cravat and the ring with a dark red stone that he wore on the little finger of his hand, which I suspected was intended to deceive the unwary observer into thinking of him as being a rather foolish fop. As far as business was concerned, he had a brisk almost curt manner that was apparent in his dismissal of his chauffeur who was given half a crown and told to decamp for an hour after which time he would be needed back sharp on the dot, for the drive back to London.

His manner changed, however, as soon as he turned to address Holmes. His voice took on a languid drawl and his vocabulary blossomed with exotic foreign epithets, mostly French, like a garden coming suddenly into bloom.

Holmes, who was evidently used to Pike's method of dealing with his business affairs poured him a large glass of port and seated him at the head of the table while he and I each took a chair at his side.

'Now,' said Pike, opening a stylish leather case which bore his monogram in gold letters and taking out a notebook, 'the Lockharts. Your contact at Barton, Lionel Larkin, was quite loquacious about them. According to him they are a well-to-do family who have been farming their land for generations. But after that, he had very little to say, apart from giving me a dissertation of his own genealogical connections with some minor gentry whom I have never heard of who live in Orpington, of all places. So,' he continued, opening his notebook with a business-like efficiency and flattening the first page with the palm of his hand, 'I took your advice and went to Birmingham, a great improvement on Barton, where I acquired some very useful information.'

Of course! I said to myself. Hetty had been living in Birmingham with her daughter Eleanor after her marriage to George Sutton and had, apparently enjoyed a busy social life among Sutton's friends. I could now see what Holmes had meant by 'a second location'. We had been concentrating too closely on Hetty's childhood and her Sussex connections. The shift away to Birmingham had opened up a whole new area of investigation.

Langdale Pike was saying, 'I spoke in particular to one lady, a Mrs William Hardy, quite an amiable person who claimed to be a *bonne amie* of Mrs Sutton. They used to go shopping *en concert*. Their children were also playmates and took their puppies out for walks together. Do you want the names?' he added, tapping his notebook. 'I have all of them here, including the puppies. You did tell me to collect as much information as possible.'

It was said in a pert manner as if Pike was getting his own back for being given the assignment in the first place, which he considered a waste of his own valuable time.

Holmes, wisely, took no notice.

'There is no need, thank you, Langdale,' he said politely. 'Go forward, if you please, to George Sutton's death. I understand Mrs Sutton took it badly.'

'Oh that, yes. Mrs Hardy mentioned that at some length, rather like Lionel Larkin and his antecedents. But Mrs Hardy's role was rather more like Florence Nightingale's, a nursemaid's.' He stopped and, rather surprisingly, looked a little abashed. 'No, that is not quite fair to the woman. I think she was genuinely fond of Mrs Sutton and her daughter and wanted to help them. She visited her quite often to make sure the staff were looking after her.'

'Staff?' Holmes repeated in a disinterested tone of voice that I knew from experience, disguised a strong, genuine curiosity, 'how many did she have?'

'About seven, I suppose,' Langdale Pike replied. 'Her husband had been quite *riche* and there were several servants, I believe: a housekeeper, a couple of maids, gardeners, a cook, of course, and a chauffeur.'

'What was his name?' Holmes asked in that same offhand voice.

'My dear man, I have no idea. Dogs are another matter – I like dogs – but servants! I hardly ever take notice of other people's domestic staff. Their lives are much too dull to cause any scandal unless the butler seduces the lady of the house or the cook poisons the dinner guests. It is their peccadillos that interest me. They are my bread and butter, my *raison d'être*. Now if you had asked about Hetty Sutton's gentleman friend, I might have been able to help you.'

Holmes immediately sat up, alert and attentive.

'A gentleman friend!' he exclaimed.

'Yes, and a most unfortunate choice as well. Some women are so *ingénue* when choosing a lover. Certainly, Hetty Sutton was, much to her misfortune.'

'Tell me about him!'

'I will tell you everything my little bird, Mrs Hardy, told me, so the juicier items may have been deleted before they came to me. You must bear that in mind. I suppose you will want to know his name?'

'You know it?' Holmes demanded.

Langdale Pike smiled in a smug know-all manner. 'Indeed I do, Sherlock. It is Roger Sinclair.'

'How did she meet him?'

'I know that, too. He was introduced to the Suttons at one of their *soirées*, before George Sutton's death, by a friend. He was from London but evidently came to Birmingham quite often, on "business", he said although he never made it clear exactly what his "business" was. I have my suspicions though. However, to *revenir à nos moutons* as the French say, he became part of the Sutton's *coterie*, a charming, amusing, good-looking addition apparently.

'Don't ask me what he did for a living; I don't know. But I imagine it was something not exactly illicit but very close to it: gambling, dealing in stocks and shares, that sort of enterprise, although, if I read the cards correctly, his main source of income was older women who fell for his charms and whom he milked, but very discreetly, mind you, to pay for his upkeep.

'However, Sinclair had his own Achilles' heel in the shape of a very beautiful and desirable woman of easy virtue, the type we English label with all sorts of crude-sounding epithets such as harlot, strumpet, whore; ugly words, you must agree, whereas the French vocabulary is much more refined and agreeable: *une grande horizontale*, for example, or a *poule de luxe*. Her name, you were about to ask?' Langdale Pike asked, casting an inquisitive, bright-eyed glance in our direction. Receiving no response, he continued, 'Her real name, I gather, was Margaret White, the youngest daughter of a minor clergyman from Stafford. Professionally, she was known as Marguerite Le Blanc. You're surely not thinking of contacting her, are you, Sherlock? I warn you she would be far outside your financial sphere, my dear man.'

Ignoring Pike's last jibe, Holmes remarked, 'I think we can guess what happened after George Sutton's death. Roger Sinclair married his widow. Before 1870, I imagine?'

I was about to ask why the choice of that particular date when its significance dawned on me. It was, of course, the year when the Married Woman's Property Act was passed in Parliament by which wives gained control of any money or assets in their names, which until that date had passed automatically into their husbands' possession.

'My dear man, need you ask?' Pike replied. 'Roger Sinclair had summed up the situation before Sutton's death. A young wife, a wealthy but elderly husband. It was only a matter of waiting, fingers crossed, for the likely outcome. No wonder Sinclair kept calling in on them in Birmingham. Like a vulture he was watching his prey, ready to move in for the kill when the time was ripe.'

Holmes looked grim.

'How much did he take?'

'Almost everything,' Langdale replied with a shrug. 'All the money and property George Sutton had left her and the child: the house, its contents, her jewellery. Need I go on? He kept the car, of course; it was a very useful status symbol. But the servants had to go. Mrs Sutton could no longer afford to keep them.'

'All of them?' Holmes asked.

'I believe so.'

'So she was left with nothing?'

'Practically nothing although I understand her mother had left her a modest inheritance in trust, so Sinclair could not get his sticky fingers on that. I suppose her mother assumed she would be more than comfortably supported by Sutton's wealth. Apparently the dear lady was ignorant of the Roger Sinclairs of this world.

'Then there was the child, of course.'

'Child?' I put in. 'You mean Eleanor, Hetty's daughter by George Sutton?'

'Actually, no. I was referring to Roger Sinclair's child. She became *enceinte* soon after the wedding.'

'Oh no!' I protested aghast.

Holmes response was much more down to earth.

'What happened to it?' he asked abruptly.

'According to my little bird, Mrs Hardy, the mother miscarried after which she had some sort of nervous breakdown. Mrs Hardy had too much *politesse* to tell me all the intimate details. By this time, Sinclair was living most of the time in London and rarely came to Birmingham.'

'And his wife?' Holmes asked.

'After the house was sold, she moved into a small rented property in the poorer part of town and lost touch with her circle of well-to-do friends, or rather they lost touch with her. My little bird, Mrs Hardy, called on her a few times but found the experience too *mélancolique* so she, too, dropped out. I think they were ashamed of her: no money, no servants, no motor car, a thoroughly unsuitable *roué* of a husband and a dead baby to boot – and in a strange way were afraid that her ill fortune was infectious and might taint theirs. After that, Mrs Sinclair disappeared, it was assumed to her parents' home somewhere in the depths of Sussex, I believe.'

Langdale Pike broke off at this point and then added, 'Is that all, Sherlock? Grateful as I am for your introduction to Lady Agatha, there is a limit to my generosity, you know. I really feel I have paid my dues. Anyway, the hour is nearly up and my driver should be here at any moment. So pour me another glass of port, my dear fellow, and let us consider the debt settled.'

As if on cue, the man arrived just as Holmes was serving the wine but, leaving him to wait on the doorstep, Pike raised his glass in a farewell salutation.

'To you, Sherlock and you, too, Dr Watson. I wish you a successful outcome to your little mystery. Do let me know the *dénouement*.'

'*Dénouement!*' Holmes exclaimed in disgust as the door closed behind Pike and we heard the car drive away. 'We are still only halfway there!'

'Are we?' I asked. 'I thought Langdale Pike was most helpful.'

'As far as he could,' Holmes agreed a little reluctantly. 'But like the business with women not appearing in genealogies, Pike has failed to mention one very important person, crucial to our investigation.'

'Did he? Who was that?'

'Work it out for yourself, Watson. And while you are doing so, give some thought to the reason why Inspector Bardle has not yet identified those fingerprints I gave him. That is another little puzzle that still has to be solved.'

CHAPTER TEN

The following day, Holmes was in a restless mood, partly due to impatience at not receiving the report from Inspector Bardle on the fingerprints found on the pantry window at Melchett Manor but mostly, I thought, through the lack of progress generally in the inquiry. But that was not all. I could tell by his mannerisms that he had some deeper problem on his mind, such as his renewed drumming with his fingertips on the table or rising abruptly from his chair to walk up and down the room suggested. More troubling was his resumption of his night-time excursions, indicating his inability to sleep. In the next two days, I heard him creeping down the stairs in the early hours of the morning, one particular tread's creaking giving him away.

I knew instinctively where he was going: to the cove to sit on that cussed rock that had began to antagonise me so deeply that I wished the wretched thing was at the bottom of the sea. It was time, I decided, that this particular mystery, and Holmes' need to keep revisiting it, should be solved once and for all.

Therefore, on the third night, when I again heard him let himself out of the house, instead of remaining in bed, fuming, I, too, went downstairs but on a more mundane mission. Lighting the lamp, I poured myself out a whisky from the tantalus on the sideboard and seated myself in one of the armchairs, glass in hand, to await Holmes' return.

According to the clock on the mantelpiece, it was three o'clock before he eventually arrived, clearly prepared by the light in the window to expect my presence and to meet me face-to-face.

'Well, Watson,' he said, looking a little chastened. 'What got you up at this ungodly hour?'

'I could ask the same of you,' I replied. 'What makes *you* get up at the same ungodly hour and go down to the cove?'

'Oh!' he exclaimed, much taken aback by my rejoinder. 'How did you find that out?'

'By following you,' I retorted.

'I see,' he said, adding with one of his quirky smiles. 'May I join you with a whisky, my dear Watson?'

'Help yourself. It's your whisky,' I replied.

I watched him cross the room to the sideboard where he rattled about for a few seconds finding a glass and opening the tantalus without speaking. However, the language of the body sometimes can convey as much, if not more, than the spoken word, and Holmes' back, at that moment, expressed a great deal. His spine stiffened and his shoulders also grew taut as he thought over the situation and how best to handle it. And then he made up his mind. His head went up and he turned to face me.

'I'm sorry,' he began.

But by this time, I was in no mood to compromise.

'Never mind the apologies,' I said. 'I would prefer an explanation, and I think I deserve an honest answer. You invited me here for a week's holiday but since my arrival I have been involved in a series of strange incidents, the significance of which you have failed to confide in me. If you do not wish to do so, that is your choice. My decision, however, is that unless you are prepared to trust me completely, I shall have to say goodbye and go home.

'I hope that is not the outcome of my visit. I regard you as an old, valued friend, Holmes, and will be distressed if we parted on unhappy terms.'

He was silent for what seemed a long time, although it was probably only a few seconds and in that silence I was fearful that I had angered him so much that it would bring an end to our friendship. And yet I could not regret a syllable of what I had said. I had meant every word and had I not spoken up, our friendship would have ended anyway – for it would have been founded on a false premise, lacking that mutual trust that was essential, in my eyes, at least, for a worthy relationship.

It was then that Holmes broke the silence.

'Let me show you something,' he said, getting to his feet. 'It's upstairs, I'll fetch it; I shall only be a moment getting it.'

He spoke in a low voice that was devoid of any stress or emotion, before leaving the room, returning shortly afterwards with a small leather box in his hand that might have contained a piece of jewellery or a watch. This he placed on the table in front of me, saying in the same dispassionate tone, 'Open it and see what is inside.'

I followed his bidding and, taking off the lid, revealed its contents.

It was not a watch as I had half-expected but a watch chain, curled up at the bottom of the container to which was attached a gold coin, threaded on it by a small hole that had been drilled in its upper rim, turning it into a decorative fob. Much bemused, I lifted it out and let it dangle between my fingers where it spun gently to and fro. It was a sovereign, I noticed, and it was only then that its significance dawned on me and I understood its hidden relevance.

Nineteen years earlier, on 20th March 1888[1] to be precise, a date I clearly remember for I became involved with one of Holmes' most famous cases and, on the same occasion, was reconciled with Holmes after a period of separation that had hurt me deeply. The cause in the rift in our relationship was my marriage, the details of which I shall not describe in detail except to explain that Holmes regarded it as a betrayal. As I stated at the beginning of this account, I consider my private life to be no one's business except my own and also because some aspects are irrelevant.

Suffice it to say, in those intervening years, I saw very little of Holmes. He continued with his vocation as a private consultant detective, for which by this time he was internationally renowned, while I resumed my old medical career as a family doctor from a practice I had bought in Paddington.

It was while I was returning from a visit to a patient on that particular evening that my route home took me past my former lodgings at 221B Baker Street. It was for old time's sake and, I admit, out of a kind

[1] In fact, Watson has mistaken the date. He records its happening on 20th March 1888 but he had not married at that time. Most editors have corrected the year to 1889. On occasion he was careless over facts and figures. Alternatively, it could be the typewriter who misread Dr Watson's manuscript, taking the final figure for '9' for an '8'. Some doctors are notorious for the poor legibility of their handwriting.

of nostalgic longing, that caused me to halt on the pavement to glance up at the windows of the sitting room which I had shared with Holmes in those days of our close friendship and to recall those evenings when we had sat together by the fireside, discussing his latest case. Other details were still clear in my memory: the tantalus on the sideboard, Holmes' cigars in the coal scuttle, his papers strewn about the room.

At that same moment, by sheer coincidence, Holmes walked past the window, casting his shadow across the blind so that I could see his tall, lean figure in silhouette, at which I made up my mind to call on him. To my delight, Holmes welcomed me and, to a degree, our old friendship was renewed.

It was during this visit that Holmes' client arrived for an appointment and Holmes suggested I stayed and was introduced to him.

And so I met the King of Bohemia and became associated with the scandal in the Bohemia case, which involved Irene Adler.

For those of you who are not familiar with that inquiry, I shall give a brief account of it, in particular, of Irene Adler herself, whom in my account, 'A Scandal in Bohemia', I referred to as '*the* woman' in Holmes' life.

She was an opera singer, a contralto, born in New Jersey in 1856, which means that in March 1889, the time of the events to which I have already referred, she was thirty-one. A highly talented diva, she had performed at La Scala Milan and the Imperial Opera House in Warsaw but had since retired to live in London, occasionally taking part in concerts.

It was during her career in Warsaw that she had met the King of Bohemia, who had not then succeeded to the throne but bore the title of Crown Prince.

It is not my place to divulge intimate details of their relationship. I leave that to my readers' imagination but the Crown Prince had sent her some compromising letters and they were photographed together. However, since those heady days, he had succeeded to the throne and was planning on an altogether more suitable regal marriage to the second daughter of the King of Scandinavia, Princess Clotilde.

Proud and strong-minded, and angry at being rejected, Irene Adler had threatened to send the compromising letters and photograph to the King of Scandinavia, thus ruining the King of Bohemia's hope of marrying his daughter. It was these items that the King of Bohemia wanted Holmes to retrieve so that his marriage could be achieved.

Holmes had agreed to take on the case and it was during his attempt to recover the letters and photographs that he saw Irene Adler coming out of her house in St John's Wood.

It was only a glimpse but it was enough.

His reaction is what the French rather dramatically call a *coup de foudre*, in other words, a 'thunderclap' and which we more prosaic English refer to as 'love at first sight'. In short, he was smitten.

Unlike myself, Holmes is not in the least uxorious. I can never imagine him settling down to married life: to the small day-to-day pleasures and mishaps, and what I call 'home-centred interests'. So the likelihood of his marrying Irene Adler, if such an opportunity should arise, was out of the question. All I can say is that she was the only woman he *might* have married.

Apart from being exceptionally beautiful, a woman whom men would die for, as Holmes himself stated, she was talented and, most important of all, intelligent. In fact, Holmes admitted that in his career, he had been beaten four times, but only once by a woman and that woman I am convinced was Irene Adler. I am prepared to stake my life on that.

The King of Bohemia was less complimentary about her, accusing her of having a 'soul of steel'. She may indeed have been spirited and with a mind of her own, traits that Holmes would have approved of, but one feels the King of Bohemia's comments were made out of bitterness and perhaps also sour grapes, for Irene Adler subsequently rejected him for another man: Godfrey Norton, a handsome young lawyer from the Inner Temple with whom she arranged a hasty marriage at St Monica's Church in

Edgware Road. It was on this occasion that Holmes had caught that soul-shattering glimpse of her as she hurried out of her house on the way to her wedding, which he inadvertently attended as a witness.

As payment for his services, Irene Adler, now Mrs Godfrey Norton, gave him a sovereign that Holmes there and then decided to wear on his watch chain as a memento, the very same coin that was lying in the leather box Holmes had set down in front of me on the table.

Readers who might be curious about the outcome of the scandal in Bohemia case and the subsequent fate of the King's reputation can rest assured. Although Irene Adler had removed the compromising photograph and letters, she had left a letter praising Holmes' investigative skills and making it clear that she would no longer threaten the King. Instead she left in place of the compromising photograph of them together a photograph of herself alone that Holmes claimed as a memento.

It was a successful outcome for Holmes at the time but, from my point of view, in the present situation was hardly satisfactory. It did nothing to explain the link between Irene Adler and the Lady in Black although I thought I could guess the answer.

'They looked alike!' I cried, suddenly struck by a *coup de foudre* of my own.

Holmes regarded me quizzically.

'If you are referring to the two ladies in question then you are only partly correct,' he replied. 'The likeness was not physical. It was subtler than that. But you are very near the mark, my dear fellow, and I admire your perspicacity. Yes, there was a similarity. In both cases I caught only a glimpse of them but it was enough to rouse my attention. It was something about the tilt of the head or the way they moved their hands – oh, Watson. I really cannot explain it because I myself do not know the answer. But from the moment I saw her sitting on that rock, I had to discover her secret, for I knew she had one, and it was essential I uncovered the truth.'

'I see,' I replied but I confess I only half understood what he was saying. 'That's why you invited me here.'

'Yes, but that is only part of it. I needed your presence, your down-to-earth common sense, the strength of your loyalty.' Here he broke off with an embarrassed laugh. 'Oh, Watson, it's really quite simple. I wanted you here as my friend.'

I was deeply moved and, I must admit, close to tears, but knowing that would never do, I cleared my throat and said, 'I'm happy to be of help.'

It was time to change the subject before both of us found it too uncomfortable but there was one point I had to clarify.

'If you don't mind me asking, Holmes, what happened to her?'

'To Irene Adler? I don't know. She and her husband left England soon after the wedding. I wasn't told where they went. I believe she died later although I don't know where or when or of what. Like the Lady in Black, she remains an enigma.'

And that was the end of the subject. Neither Holmes nor I ever referred to Irene Adler again. But I could not quite get her out of my mind; or rather, how the circumstances of his reaction to her reflected an aspect of Holmes personality that had troubled me for some time: his attitude to women, for that affected not only his relationship with me but also that with my wife.

In my account, 'A Scandal in Bohemia', I refer to Holmes' opinion of 'the softer passions' which he never referred to without – and I quote my own words – 'a jibe and a sneer', a slight exaggeration on my part for, when he wished, he could be courteous and charming to women. But, basically, he disliked and distrusted them. Indeed, he himself admitted he had never loved or felt any emotion that was 'akin to love'.

Generally speaking he found them trivial, untrustworthy, illogical and vain, and I often wondered how or what had caused this resentment. I am now convinced that it was due to his childhood and upbringing.

He never referred to his parents, not even his mother, and it occurred to me that it was his mother's treatment of him as a child that had nurtured his attitude to the opposite sex. Perhaps she had been selfish, vain, and untrustworthy, neglectful of her son's needs and not showing him the love and attention that children crave, so he had grown up with this huge gap in his emotional life, making him lack the ability to love.

The only family member I ever met is his older brother, Mycroft, and he also showed the same aloofness and unsociability. He, too, never married and, in his case, had no friends at all, although he showed an almost paternal attachment to Holmes, addressing him as 'my dear boy'. Otherwise he lived a solitary existence in lodgings in Pall Mall or his office in Whitehall, his only diversion being the evenings he spent at the Diogenes Club opposite his flat, and of which he was a co-founder. But even there, his hours were strictly limited from a quarter to five to twenty to eight. In addition, conversation was only allowed in the Stranger's Room, so it was not exactly a companionable venue. He hardly ever visited Holmes in Baker Street although Holmes called on him from time to time at the Diogenes.

However, Mycroft showed a brotherly interest in Holmes' career, assisting him with his more difficult cases on several occasions. Like Holmes, he was highly intelligent with a unique ability for remembering and correlating facts; a gift that Mycroft used to distinction in his role of confidential adviser to the government, so that Holmes claimed, with a show of fraternal pride, at times, Mycroft *was* the government.

This similarity in the personalities of the two brothers confirmed my suspicion that this was due to their joint upbringing rather than an individual quirk in Holmes' character and that I was correct in thinking that a lack of motherly love was to blame.

When I joined him in Fulworth, I was much relieved to discover that there had been fundamental changes in Holmes' personality. He had become, as they say, a new man and this transformation, I felt, could be put down to the loss of stress he had been subjected to in his former career as a consulting detective. I had noticed in the weeks prior to his retirement he had become more and more erratic in his behaviour, on one occasion clenching his fists and punching into the air in a fit of uncontrollable excitement, on others being depressed and low-spirited.

Now that stress had been lifted, he had become much improved although some characteristics of the old Holmes remained, for example, his impatience with Mrs B although that was understandable. She could at times be an exasperating woman. He still preserved his secretiveness as well, an example of which was demonstrated in his deception over the two packages containing our disguises for the ruse he had planned to gain access to Fulworth Hall. But much of it was simply to tease me and to amuse himself and I was used enough to his sense of humour either to tolerate or ignore it.

Since his retirement he had made new friends, and took better care of his health, swimming in the lagoons in the beach when the tide went out and taking long walks over the Downs, a change in lifestyle that, as a doctor, I thoroughly approved of. He had also given up his habit of injecting himself with cocaine – at least there was no sign of syringes lying about – and he no longer suffered from those periods of exhaustion when he would lie on the sofa for days on end, staring up at the ceiling, a symptom of the narcotic effects of the drug.

But best of all, at least in my opinion, was the change in his attitude to women, or to one woman in particular.

She is, of course, Maud Bellamy whom, Holmes stated in his own words, he would always remember, as 'a most complete and remarkable woman' referring also to her physical appearance, her 'perfect clear cut face' and 'delicate colouring'. Unlike his reaction to Irene Adler, his feelings for Maud Bellamy are those of a father or an uncle, tender and affectionate, showing none of the passionate infatuation he had shown for '*the* woman'.

This change of heart on Holmes' part gave me great hope that he would be willing to accept my wife, not as the cause of a betrayal but as a friend, and that the final gap that still existed between us would be closed for good.

I was later to discover that this hope had been fulfilled.

In our conversation about Irene Adler, I had temporarily forgotten Holmes' earlier remarks about a person missing from Langdale Pike's report on his research into the Lady in Black investigation. Holmes, too, seemed to have set it to one side for he did not refer to it again until two days later when Holmes received a telephone call, apparently expected by him, which referred to that person's name. I was delighted to discover that I had guessed correctly for it was the same individual whom I, too, had chosen.

And with that choice, as later events were to prove, the last piece of the puzzle finally dropped into place and the mystery of the Lady in Black was solved.

CHAPTER ELEVEN

There was, however, one aspect of Holmes' character that I had not taken into consideration: his tendency towards secretiveness, sometimes over the most trivial matters, such as hiding away the two parcels that contained the disguises for his stratagem to gain access to Fulworth Hall, when he could simply have told me of their contents at the time he had acquired them.

Part of this tendency arose from his innate and sometimes bizarre sense of humour, such as the time, when, having recovered the Mazarin stone known as the Crown diamond and placed it in Lord Cantlemere's safe keeping, he slipped the gem into the man's pocket, an act which his Lordship, much bewildered, regarded as 'perverse' although Holmes tried to pass it off as an 'impish' example of his love of practical jokes.

I experienced another example of his secretiveness the next day although at the time I thought little of it.

In the mornings, it had become a routine that I would start the preparations for breakfast, such as laying the table and making the toast while Holmes was busy with tasks concerning the care of his bees that usually took about ten minutes, or so.

That particular morning, I had everything ready, the breakfast china laid out, the toast and butter on the table along with the customary pot of honey but Holmes did not return and, a little surprised by his non-appearance, I opened the front door to find out what had kept him.

He was nowhere to be seen, so I retreated back to the kitchen where I had put a pan of milk on the stove to heat up, anxious that it might boil over if I left it there for too long. It was while I was in the kitchen that I heard Holmes letting himself into the sitting room.

'Oh, you're back,' I remarked, as I joined him at the table.

'Back?' he repeated. 'I was never gone, my dear fellow.'

I left the matter there. It seemed too petty to follow it up any further although it did strike me as a little odd that he had not given me even a simple explanation for his absence for those few minutes.

The following day another strange little event occurred, this time over a letter that was delivered by the morning post. As I was in the hall at the time, I picked it up from the floor and took it through to the sitting room to give it to him.

He glanced at it in a perfunctory manner and then stuffed it into his pocket without saying a word.

I found this reaction also a little unusual: most people when handed a letter would make some remark about it if only to complain, 'Oh, it's only another bill.' But Holmes said nothing and, like the business of his disappearing briefly at the previous breakfast-time, I said nothing either.

He also made no reference to his avoidance of the cove when we left the cottage for our morning outing in order to evade Mrs B's arrival. But this I could understand. Our recent conversation concerning Irene Adler had, I imagined, roused old memories that, at least for the time being, he preferred not to recall. Instead we went walking on the Downs, calling in at the Fisherman's Arms for our usual hearty midday meal of home-baked bread and cheese washed down with a glass of ale.

It was not until the third morning that this little mystery began to unravel.

We had finished breakfast when suddenly, out

of the blue, he said, 'Would you be kind enough, Watson, to drive us to Barton today?'

'Of course,' I replied. 'Is it for any particular reason?'

'As a matter of fact, it is. Do you remember me saying a little time ago that there was another person connected with our Lady in Black inquiry that we had not yet considered?'

'Yes, indeed I do, Holmes. You asked me if I would guess who it was.'

'And did you?' he asked, raising a quizzical eyebrow.

'Not a person so much as a place.'

'Which is?'

'Abbot's Farm,' I replied, wondering where this brisk little exchange was taking us. 'I thought at the time that it was worth a little more investigation. After all, it was the family home of the Lockharts and there could well be a connection.'

'Oh, well done, Watson!' Holmes exclaimed with none of his sardonic overtones, which often accompanied such praise. 'You have hit the bullseye, as they say, my dear fellow. I was thinking exactly along the same lines myself. I am certain Abbot's Farm and its inhabitants are well worth a visit.'

'Is that why you want to go to Barton this morning?'

'Another bullseye!' he cried but this time he was

being ironic, 'I'll make a private consulting detective of you yet.'

'So what are proposing Holmes? Not another little stratagem like the one we used at Fulworth Hall. Will I be expected to wear a beard this time? I mean, we can hardly just turn up without any warning.'

'That has already been settled,' he replied with an airy insouciance. 'I have arranged a meeting with them at the farm this morning. In fact we've been invited there for coffee at eleven o'clock.'

'Really?' I was astonished. 'When was all this planned?'

'Yesterday, as a matter of fact.'

'Oh, I see,' I said.

And I did indeed see; probably more than Holmes himself realised. For the little mystery surrounding his absence two days before and even the arrival of the letter and Holmes' squirrelling it away upstairs was now explained. There was a pillar box a few yards up the lane where a letter could be posted in which these arrangements were suggested and the reply was sent the following day.

But why on earth Holmes had chosen to behave with all this unnecessary secrecy had still not been satisfactorily settled.

I said, 'Why did you not tell me, Holmes?'

'About what?' he asked.

'The letters,' I replied.

'Oh, those,' he said, shrugging off my question.

'Yes, those. There's no need for you to tell me if you prefer not to.' I continued. 'But I was under the impression that we were working together to solve this Lady in Black inquiry.'

Holmes' response was to burst out laughing, not quite the reaction I had been expecting but a relief all the same.

'Oh, Watson, Watson!' he chided. 'How refreshingly frank you can be. Embarrassingly so at times. I did correspond with Mr Lockhart who is the present owner of Abbot's Farm. To be honest, I was not entirely truthful in my letter to him either. In fact, I told a downright lie, which I thought you would disapprove of, knowing your dislike of fibs. And how did I know that, you may ask? By your habit of crossing your fingers behind your back when you yourself have had to – well, shall we say obfuscate the facts? It is a gesture you probably picked up when you were a child as a sign to bring good luck or ward off evil spirits. Am I right?'

'Yes, Holmes,' I said, much abashed.

'Don't be embarrassed, my dear fellow. Everyone has some little quirk or mannerism. But to return to the business of the letters. In mine to Mr Lockhart, I asked if I might visit him in the near future as I believed there was a family connection and, as I would be in the area for only a short time, I would be grateful if a meeting could be arranged in the next few days. So, there you are, Watson. Only half-lies; not complete whoppers. Am I forgiven?'

'Of course!' I exclaimed.

'And also,' Holmes added with one of his wry smiles, 'I rather enjoy teasing you at times. Now, is there anything else you would like to know about this visit to the Lockharts?'

'Only to ask why you have decided to call on them? Do you think they have anything of importance to add to our Lady in Black inquiry?'

'Probably not, but there are one or two aspects of the case that I would like to clarify.'

'Such as?'

'They are small, minor details but worth inquiring into all the same. For example, why did Eleanor Lockhart marry Henry Trevalyan? According to Mrs B, he was a selfish man, "stuck-up", to use her expression, unpopular in the village, who disinherited his daughter because she married someone in "trade", demeaning to him because he wanted to play the role of lord of the manor. I wondered why. I also wondered why he left Cornwall, to come to Fulworth. According to that little pamphlet in the church, he came from a well-to-do family, owners of a tin mining company. So what persuaded him to pack up and leave? Was it on his own volition or was he pushed? I feel there's another mystery buried there.

'I am finding genealogy a fascinating subject, despite people like Lionel Larkin poking about in their own ancestry hoping to find some noble forbears to compensate for their own insignificance. I enjoy it for the simple reason one can learn a lot about *people*: their lives, their hopes and fears, their triumphs and disasters. It is like peeling off the skin of an orange to get to the juicy heart of the fruit.'

At this point, he unexpectedly burst out laughing again.

'And to be perfectly frank, my dear Watson – and no finger-crossing is needed here – I am by nature a very inquisitive person who likes to uncover other people's secrets. That is why I became a private consulting detective. It is part nosiness and part wanting to ferret out the truth.

'I think we both know by now the identity of the Lady in Black. But that is only a name. What we don't know is much more interesting. What drives her to sit on a rock in the middle of the night and look out to sea? That's why I want to go to Abbot's Farm. The answer may lie there. So are you game?'

'Of course I am,' I answered him stoutly.

'Good old Watson! So shall we go?' Holding up his right hand with mock solemnity, the index and middle fingers crossed, he added, 'Let us hope we don't meet Lionel Larkin on the way.'

There was no sign of him as we drove into Barton

so as Holmes pointed out with a sardonic smile, the cross-fingered gesture must have worked.

'I shall have to start using it myself in this investigation,' he remarked. 'Perhaps our luck will turn for the good there as well.'

It had certainly given us a perfect day of bright sunshine and a light breeze that stirred the leaves, bringing us the aroma of warm earth and grass. Under a blue sky, faintly marbled here and there with white clouds, Abbot's Farm lay at peace.

It was the first time we had seen the place at close range having viewed it before only from the lane, so as we approached it up the driveway I was aware of another side to it, apart from its unspoilt beauty. It was a working farm. There were barns and outbuildings, a milking parlour and a chicken house, the inhabitants of which were pecking about the yard and scattered in a flurry of feathers as we arrived.

There were other signs of activity as well: the sound of a thresher in some distant field, the deep-throated lowing of cows and the barking of a dog, a beautiful black, flop-eared spaniel that came running out of the house to meet us, and after sniffing at us suspiciously decided we were acceptable and wagged its tail in greeting.

Behind the dog came a pleasant-faced, middle-aged man who, like the dog, was willing to make friends as he held out his hand in welcome.

'Mr Holmes and Dr Watson?' he asked. 'Pleased to meet you both. I'm Bob Lockhart. And this,' he added, rubbing the top of the dog's head, 'is Peggy. Do come in.'

He stood aside to let us pass into a large, square hall, part of the original Tudor building, I guessed, judging by the beamed ceiling and the stone slabs on the floor. It had a subtle, complex aroma of smoke from log fires that had permeated the very wood and plaster of the place, mingled with the homely smell of baking bread and the sweeter scent of flowers and herbs wafting in from the garden.

'I think the best person for you to see is my father, Tom,' Bob Lockhart was saying. 'He was a boy when Hetty Sutton used to visit here. He'll be better able to tell you more about the family at that time than I can.'

As he spoke, he ushered us across the hall and down a passage that led off it, stopping at a door halfway down to add, 'My wife will bring you coffee shortly. My father won't join you. He's old, you see, and has the shakes in his hands so he gets embarrassed about eating and drinking anything in front of other people.'

Knocking on the door, he opened it to announce, 'It's me, Dad. I've brought Mr Holmes and Dr Watson to meet you. I told you about them yesterday? They knew Hetty. Remember her? Hetty?'

He was addressing an elderly, white-haired man who sat in a winged armchair by the window, a plaid rug over his knees despite the warmth from the sunlight that poured into the room.

For a few seconds, he looked across at us, summing us up as the dog had done, before accepting us. We evidently passed muster for he nodded and then beckoned us into the room while his son hurriedly moved two chairs forward for us to sit on.

Although old, he had still kept an interest in life, unlike some elderly patients I had doctored in my time. His expression was alert and his eyes, a surprising bright blue, regarded us from under a thatch of white hair with a keen gaze. There were signs about him of his younger, outdoor life as a farmer in his weathered skin and the many small wrinkles gathered round his eyes and across his forehead from working outside in the wind or the bright light of the sun. It was there, too, in his hands, the tendons of which were gnarled like the roots of a tree holding firmly to the soil in which it grew. It was only the tremor in them as they lay side by side on top of the plaid rug that suggested he suffered from any physical weakness.

Turning his head to address his son, he said sharply, 'Hetty? Of course I remember her. I may be old but I'm not senile yet.'

Bob Lockhart grinned at this rejoinder, amused by his father's outspokenness and nodded to us to indicate it was only good-humoured family banter, not to be taken seriously.

'Then I'll leave you to it,' he replied, as he left the room.

'So you knew Hetty?' old Mr Lockhart said as Holmes and I sat down on the chairs facing him.

I glanced across at Holmes, wondering how he was going to respond to this direct approach or whether it would become another fingers-crossed situation, but he seemed relaxed as if he were enjoying the encounter. Certainly he and old Mr Lockhart seemed to have come to some unspoken, friendly agreement at their meeting.

'I knew *of* her,' Holmes replied. 'I was told she used to come here with her daughter.'

'Ah, little Eleanor,' old Mr Lockhart said, his tone full of warmth. 'She was a real little beauty. Named after her grandmother, of course. It was an old family name. My father, Robert, was her cousin. Us Lockharts tend to do the same. Hetty was named after *her* father, Henry Trevalyan. Did you know him?'

'No, I never met him,' Holmes replied.

'Then thank your lucky stars,' old Mr Lockhart replied, a totally unexpected response. 'No one in the family liked him. In fact, grandma Ellie cried when Eleanor said she was getting engaged to him. She was going to marry David Selby, a nice young man; had a farm over at Lower Melchett.'

'Lower Melchett!' Holmes exclaimed.

'You know it?' Old Mr Lockhart asked.

'As a matter of fact, I called in at Melchett Manor once,' Holmes said, not quite a finger-crossing situation for it was perfectly true; Holmes had indeed called in there.

'Did you meet Sir Oliver Wayne?' Old Mr Lockhart asked eagerly, obviously delighted that this bond had been formed between Holmes and himself. It was then I realised what was happening. The old man had misunderstood Holmes' role in the situation. He had taken it to be a more intimate relationship than it really was, with mutual friends and acquaintances; almost family, in fact, and therefore it was quite permissible to confide personal details that he would probably not have shared with a stranger.

He was an elderly man, almost certainly lonely, whose own family was too busy to spend much time reminiscing about the past. So to him, Holmes was a godsend, a willing listener to the kind of past recollections that his own son was too busy to pay attention to.

I glanced across at Holmes, wondering if he, too, was aware of this. I could tell by the way he met my gaze that he knew what he was doing. There was a certain cocking of his head to the right telling me: 'Yes, I know what you are thinking,' and an almost imperceptible raising of his left eyebrow that warned me not to do anything about it. So old Mr Lockhart was left to continue his assumption that we were not quite what he thought we were, and so he chatted on.

He was asking Holmes about his relationship with Sir Oliver Wayne. Had he met him at Melchett Manor?

'No,' Holmes replied, quite truthfully. 'I believe he and his wife, Lady Wayne, were on holiday in Italy at the time.'

'That's when the burglars broke in and stole some of their silver,' old Mr Lockhart informed us. 'Dreadful business!'

'Yes, indeed,' Holmes agreed solemnly. 'Quite awful.'

Neither of them spoke for a few moments, as they both considered the depravity of such an act, like the two-minute silence that follows a public memorial service. Then, the mourning over, old Mr Lockhart picked up the conversation where he had left it.

'Eleanor's fiancé, David Selby – you remember I mentioned him? – he asked to go hunting with Sir Oliver's father. That's what killed him. He was thrown off his horse one Friday when they were out with the hounds; broke his neck.'

Holmes and I both made suitably shocked responses, which old Mr Lockhart acknowledged with a nod of his head, before he continued with his narrative.

'That's when Henry Trevalyan took over. She was caught on the rebound, so to speak; still grieving over David. He'd met her at some village do or other, and he used to come calling, all smarmy and lovey-dovey.'

I assumed he was referring to Henry Trevalyan although one had to read between the pronouns to make exact sense of what he was saying.

Holmes, who seemed to be having no problem, remarked casually, 'He came from Cornwall, didn't he?'

'That's right. Tin mining.'

It was said dismissively, as if Cornwall and tin mining were well outside old Mr Lockhart's scope of interest.

'Why on earth did he come to Fulworth? It seems a strange choice to make,' Holmes replied.

'According to my father, he wanted to be a gentleman, someone who doesn't have to get his hands dirty to make a living. As I understood it, it was his older brother who owned the mine and made all the decisions. He didn't like that. So he sold his share of the business, put the proceeds into the bank and came here to live on the interest. No one knew him down here, you see, so he could act the gentleman with not a soul to question his right. My father always said it was the same need to be part of the gentry that persuaded Henry Trevalyan to marry Eleanor; her husband-to-be – David Selby – was a friend of Sir Francis Wayne, Sir Oliver's grandfather, so that to Henry Trevalyan was almost as good as a ticket to the House of Lords. Don't ask me why Eleanor agreed to marry *him*. She was a woman, so God alone knows the answer to that one.'

Loneliness, I thought, was a possible explanation but I said nothing. Anyway, the conversation was cut short at this point by a tap on the door, heralding the arrival of his daughter-in-law, Mrs Lockhart, bearing a tray of coffee cups, the complementary milk jug and sugar basin, and a plate of home-made shortbread biscuits. It was as if the bond between Holmes and the old Mr Lockhart, as well as their conversation, was immediately severed. Old Mr Lockhart sank back into his chair, and his hands began to shake more visibly as Mrs Lockhart, not a direct member of the family, and of another generation, bustled about smiling and passing cups of coffee and biscuits to her guests while he took a back seat.

The talk moved to less personal topics to which old Mr Lockhart made slow responses apart from an occasional nod of his head or an enigmatic 'oh-ah' that I took to be a form of partial agreement.

We took our leave shortly afterwards, Mr and Mrs Lockhart and Peggy, the dog, accompanying us to the front door where Holmes and I said our farewells, old Mr Lockhart remaining in his chair by the window.

'Any use?' I enquired of Holmes as we set off down the drive on the way home: meaning, had the encounter with the Lockharts produced any significant evidence in the Lady in Black investigation.

There was a long silence before he replied, and when he finally spoke it was with obvious reluctance.

'Only that one should be very, very careful whom one chooses to be one's parents.'

'But one can't choose, Holmes!' I protested.

'Exactly so, my dear fellow,' Holmes replied. 'With your usual perspicacity, you have again struck the nail on the head.'

And with that he said nothing more during the whole journey back to Fulworth, leaving me wondering quite what to make of his reply and whether or not it had any relevance to the Lady in Black inquiry.

CHAPTER TWELVE

Holmes was in a very subdued state of mind for the next few days and seemed reluctant to discuss the Lady in Black inquiry so, respecting his silence, I made no reference to either the case nor his mood even though I thought I had found the answer to his remark concerning the missing person in Langdale Pike's account which I was eager to discuss with him.

As for Inspector Bardle's failure in sending any report on the fingerprints on the pantry window in Melchett Manor, there was nothing I could do or say regarding this matter, although we learnt later by post that he had been called in to assist in a case of fraud in Lewes, which had temporarily taken up his time. However, as soon as it was cleared up, he had been able to turn his attention to Holmes' inquiry regarding the fingerprint evidence, a report on which he had included in his letter.

Unfortunately, it was not the outcome Holmes had anticipated for, having eagerly torn open the envelope and scanned its contents, he crumpled up both and tossed them into the grate in disgust.

'Not good news?' I asked.

'No, Watson; not good at all. The prints on the visiting card I handed to that manservant at Fulworth Hall did *not* match those found in Melchett Manor. Had they been the same, the case would have been solved.'

'Oh, I am so sorry, Holmes,' I said, knowing how much it meant to him.

He gave me one of his lopsided smiles.

'I agree it is a setback but not the end of the world. What does that old axiom say: "If at first you don't succeed, try, try, try again." To be frank, I find its advice infuriating and, in this instance, quite inappropriate. We can't try again or rather, can't use the same stratagem and turn up at Fulworth Hall for a second time pretending to be an American bibliophile and his chauffeur. So I shall have to put my mind to the problem and conjure up some other little ruse although at the moment I can think of nothing.'

'I am sure you will, Holmes,' I said positively in an attempt to raise his spirits.

'My dear, Watson,' he replied, 'thank you for your support. You are a good friend to me, you know. I am very fortunate.'

I was deeply moved by the sincerity in his voice and would have done anything to help him although I realised only Holmes could find the answer to this particular problem.

He was saying, 'I know why the business over the fingerprint failed. The wrong person took hold of the card. But say no more about it. There must be more interesting matters we can discuss.'

'Yes, of course, Holmes,' I agreed, adding, in the hope that a change of subject might cheer him up, 'By the way, I think I know what you meant about the person who was missing from Langdale Pike's account.'

'Really?' Holmes asked. I thought I saw a momentary brightening of his eyes, so I pressed on.

'It was Eleanor, wasn't it? Hetty's daughter by George Sutton.'

He was silent for several seconds and I was afraid I had thrust him into even deeper despondency. And then he lifted his hand and I saw that small wry smile touch the corner of his lips again.

'Oh well done, Watson!' he exclaimed in a sardonic tone of voice so I knew he had recovered his spirits. 'You are quite right, of course. Langdale Pike and Lionel Larkin suffer from the same mental handicap: a fixed perception of people, their feelings, their relationships, their very view of the world. Like horses, they are wearing blinkers and their visual awareness is restricted. In other words, they suffer from a form of tunnel vision. In Lionel Larkin's case, it was to see genealogy entirely from a masculine point of view. In Langdale Pike's, it is the adult who is supreme. Children play no role in his view of the world, only the grown-ups.

'So you are right, dear fellow. How old was Eleanor Sutton when her mother married Sinclair? Five years old or thereabouts; a crucial age in a child's development, when she is beginning to become more self-aware and her perceptions of the world about her are maturing. And what did she see? Her father dead and replaced by an uncaring stepfather, her mother on the verge of a breakdown, her home broken up, the friends she had once known no longer there. It must have had a dreadful effect on her. Roger Sinclair has a great deal to answer for. One can only hope he pays a high price for all the damage he has done. But I think that is too much to ask. People like Sinclair tend to sail through life untouched by any feelings of guilt, their consciences intact; that is if they possess one.'

'And we can do nothing,' I said, deeply moved by Holmes' comments.

'Not unless you happen to possess a magic wand,' he replied. Then suddenly his mood shifted. 'Oh come, my dear fellow!' he exclaimed. 'We cannot continue in this doleful manner. Let us find a more cheerful subject to discuss. What about Harold Stackhurst's party on Saturday evening? Now there's an event to look forward to. May I suggest I leave you to supply the flowers while I order the champagne?'

And so the gloom lifted, at least for the time being although I still had the uneasy feeling that it was merely lurking in a dark corner ready to creep out again should either of us give it the opportunity.

We were a little late in setting out for The Gables on Saturday evening. There had been a heavy rainfall in the night that had affected the car's ignition and I had some difficulty in getting it to start. By the time we arrived, Holmes bearing the champagne and I the flowers, the party had begun in the large drawing room that overlooked the garden and the Downs at the back of the house. Pausing in the doorway for a moment to inspect the guests already present, I noticed several whom I recognised, among them Ian Murdoch, at the sight of whom my heart sank a little, remembering the awkward situation that had arisen the last time we had met him. But it lifted again when I saw Maud Bellamy was not with him. She was standing some distance away, looking more beautiful than I remembered, wearing a dark blue dress, the colour of amethysts, her russet-coloured hair swept back into what I believe is called a chignon. Harold Stackhurst was there, too, of course on the far side of the room.

There were several more guests whom I took to be the other members of Stackhurst's staff including his housekeeper, Mrs Dobson, who had answered the doorbell and ushered us into the room. Among the others were two complete strangers whom I had never met before and whose presence there I could not account for. Both of them were men, both strongly built, both red-haired, whom I took to be father and son, the older of whom sported a beard, the younger clean-shaven. Although smartly dressed in well-cut suits, they looked ill at ease, as if unused to such formal attire or such a social occasion.

I also searched hurriedly for any ladies present who might be Stackhurst's bride-to-be but could find no one who seemed at all a likely choice. There was Mrs Dobson, of course, a pleasant enough lady but rather heavy about the hips, and another member of staff who, I had been told, dealt with the secretarial duties at the academy but who could not be a candidate being in her late fifties, and, more to the point, married to the owner of the post office in Fulworth.

So who on earth could she be?

At this moment, Harold Stackhurst saw us standing in the doorway and, setting aside his glass, hurried across the room to greet us.

'I am so sorry we are late,' Holmes said as the three of us shook hands all round.

'The car wouldn't start,' I added in explanation.

'But you are here now and that is all that matters. And now,' he continued, turning his head to address someone who had approached him from behind, 'let me introduce you to my wife-to-be, although you already know her.'

Holmes and I looked beyond him and we both gaped in astonishment; at least I did. For standing behind him, a smile on her lips and her hand held out in greeting was Maud Bellamy.

For a moment, I could not believe my eyes. Maud Bellamy! That beautiful young woman! My astonishment quickly changed to delight and relief.

Holmes, who was in better control of the situation than I was, stepped forward and lifted her hand to his lips in a chivalrous salutation such as a courtier might bestow on his queen.

'Congratulations!' he exclaimed. 'What wonderful news!'

I repeated his words but not the gesture, feeling I did not know her as personally as Holmes and aware that I lacked his ability to be charming to women when he wished.

She gave us both a smile that I can only describe as radiant, lighting up her features as the dazzle from a ray of sunlight can illuminate a room. Harold

Stackhurst's happiness was also evident but, as a man whom I suspected was not used to displaying his emotions, his was a steady glow at which I felt one could warm one's hands as well as one's heart.

Maud Bellamy was saying, 'Thank you so much for the beautiful bouquet. Red roses! Did you know they are the symbol of love in the language of flowers?'

I did, in fact, know it. My own wife had taught me that when I had given her the same flowers on our engagement.

'And thank you also for the champagne,' Stackhurst was adding. 'We shall drink to the health of both of you. And now,' he continued, leading the way across the room towards the two red-haired men I had noticed when we first arrived, 'allow me to introduce Tom Bellamy, Maud's father, and her brother, William. Of course,' he continued, turning to them, 'you have both met Sherlock Holmes but not Dr John Watson, a friend of his who is at present visiting Fulworth.'

There followed communal shaking of hands and exchange of comments about the wedding-to-be, congratulations on the part of Holmes and myself for their being related to the prospective bride and thanks from the Bellamys, which I thought were not as hearty as they might have been, before we moved on to one of those conversations that tend to occur on such occasions with the participants doing their best to find a topic that suited everyone, like trying on hats, I always think, hoping to find one that fits. In this case, it was the beauty of the area, particularly the coast with its magnificent cliffs before we moved away to speak to other guests in the room.

It was a very pleasant evening that everyone seemed to enjoy, even Ian Murdoch whose possible reactions to the engagement had caused me some concern. Yet speaking to him later after an excellent buffet supper, he seemed quite reconciled to the situation, much to my relief.

I raised the subject with Holmes on the drive back from The Gables but he seemed quite sanguine about it.

'You fret too much about other people,' he told me.

'Perhaps I do,' I agreed. 'I am afraid it is in my nature.'

'Then learn to conquer it,' he advised, easy enough for him to say as he had a much more objective attitude to life than I possessed.

'I shall try,' I promised but could not resist adding, 'What about the Bellamys? They did not seem too pleased about the engagement.'

'There you go again, my dear fellow! Taking other people's troubles onto your own shoulders. They, too, will have to learn, which will be difficult for them, I imagine. They are both so positively male with a predilection for controlling others. But I think they will have met their match in Maud Bellamy and Harold. Neither of them will submit to any form of bullying; you can take my word for that.

'All the same, they are a very interesting couple: the Bellamys, I mean, and one can't help admiring them. Tom Bellamy in particular. He started off as an ordinary fisherman renting one of those small cottages by the harbour in Fulworth. Then, as I think I have already told you, the fishing trade began to die out due to the railway failing to extend this far. As a result, the whole community declined and many of its members left, literally to fish in more productive waters, such as Brighton. But Tom Bellamy stayed on and built up a little business of his own, very modest to begin with, such as taking holiday visitors for trips around the bay. And it worked. Soon he was renting out boats and bathing huts. Later, he took on his son as a partner in the business. Between them, they have made a small fortune, enough for Tom Bellamy to afford to build his own house on that slope of rising ground behind the village, the one with the tower on its corner called The Haven. You may have noticed it.'

'Indeed I have. It's quite imposing.'

'A touch pretentious perhaps,' Holmes suggested. 'But I suppose Bellamy has every right to advertise his success. He has worked hard enough for it.'

'I wonder when the wedding will take place,' I remarked.

'They seem not to have fixed a date yet. But if Tom Bellamy has anything to do with it, you can be certain it will be a splendid event with no expense spared,' Holmes prophesied.

He was proved to be right.

To jump forward in time, the ceremony took place on the fifth of May in the following summer at St Botolph's, a more magnificent setting than the smaller, brick-and-tile church that had replaced it in the village.

My wife and I were both invited to the wedding but unfortunately, one of my patients fell seriously ill at the time and I could not attend. My wife, however, was there and gave me a full account of the event that same evening over the telephone.

St Botolph's was packed, she told me, with a large congregation and was beautifully decorated with lilies and red roses, a detail that pleased me greatly, while the ceremony itself was quite simple. Her father gave her away, her brother William acting as best man. Holmes was one of the ushers together with Ian Murdoch.

'Did the church smell damp?' I asked, remembering the unpleasant odour of rotting plaster that had tainted the air when Holmes and I had last visited the place.

'Damp!' my wife replied, as if astonished by my remark. 'Not at all. It smelt of flowers; quite delicious.'

It crossed my mind that the presence of people within the building was all the church needed to dispel that miasma of decay, as if the stones themselves responded to their warmth and admiration.

But before I could carry this rather bizarre thought any further, my wife was continuing with her own more conventional account.

There were no bridesmaids, however, she added. An omission she seemed sorry to have to report. I guessed Maud herself may have made this decision, overriding her father's more lavish desire for a bevy of overdressed maids-in-waiting.

The bride's gown, however, had delighted her and, like most women, she felt it necessary to describe the garment in detail. It was white silk, beautifully fitted, with a small train, and she also wore a lace veil over her hair, held in place by a coronet of lilies of the valley, the same flower that composed her bouquet.

The reception was held in the drawing room of The Gables together with a marquee in the garden.

But what delighted me most was her account of Holmes' part in the event, an aspect of the occasion that, remembering his reaction to my second marriage, had caused me some uneasiness. However, it seemed Holmes could not have been more kind and amiable to her. He had arranged for a hired car to take her not only from the station in Brighton but also to the hotel in Lewes where he had booked a room for her for the night and, as my wife added, he had acted as her escort throughout the whole day.

So there were two happy endings, I told myself.

However, no such conclusion, happy or otherwise, occurred to bring the Lady in Black inquiry to a satisfactory conclusion, much to Holmes' displeasure, and to mine as well.

The days were passing and the supposed week's holiday had extended itself to a longer and longer period of absenteeism. I felt it was time to go home, not just for my patients' sake and my wife's but for mine as well. Nevertheless, I hesitated to break the news to Holmes.

He, too, was having a difficult time. The lack of success over the Lady in Black investigation had set him back, plunging him into one of those dark moods that had in the past overwhelmed him on occasions and I was loath to leave him in such a low state of mind.

'I feel I have reached a dead end,' he confided in me over breakfast one morning. 'Perhaps I ought to admit defeat and give the whole business up.'

'Oh, not yet, Holmes,' I protested, knowing how much it meant to him. 'Your luck may change.'

'Luck!' he retorted. 'You are beginning to sound like Mrs B chattering on about silver linings and guardian angels. No, Watson! Life isn't like that. As we both know only too well, what we need for this case is proof and I have not found it. So I have failed. There is no avoiding the issue. I will have to learn to accept it. Please leave the matter there, my dear fellow. There is no point in discussing it any further.'

And that, I knew, was that. Holmes had made up his mind and I would have to accept his decision. It seemed the case of the Lady in Black was over and done with.

CHAPTER THIRTEEN

But I was to be proved wrong, thank goodness. There was an end to it after all but whether guardian angels or silver linings had anything to do with it, I do not know.

It happened three days later quite unexpectedly and not at all as either of us might have expected.

At about nine o'clock on the Tuesday evening following Maud Bellamy's and Harold Stackhurst's engagement party, there came a loud knocking at the front door. As Holmes rose from his chair to answer it, he lifted an inquiring eyebrow at me. We expected no one and it was quite late at night for visitors to call.

I heard voices in the hall, that of Holmes and of

another man who spoke with a north-country accent, which I did not recognise but who evidently had some urgent business with my old friend, judging by his tone of voice and the speed with which Holmes ushered him into the room.

He was a stockily built, grey-haired man, elderly but still strong about the chest and shoulders, wearing a shabby tweed jacket and carrying a flat cap, also well worn. I thought I had seen him before but for a moment I could not remember where or when I might have met him. He certainly did not recognise me for no sooner had he entered than he turned immediately to Holmes.

'You must come at once, Doctor!' he exclaimed, his weather-beaten features distorted with distress.

'I am not the doctor,' Holmes told him, adding as he indicated me, 'but my friend Dr Watson is. And you are?'

'Neave,' the man replied. 'Bill Neave.'

He spoke hurriedly as if the business of exchanging names was of no importance. Turning to address me, he continued. 'She's ill, doctor! Very ill. I think she's dying. Please, you've got to come at once! *Please!*'

The words came tumbling out, his voice becoming more hoarse and broken with each disjointed sentence. As he repeated the last word, he began to weep, dashing away the tears with the back of his hand.

I find it distressing enough to see a woman cry but to witness a man, and an elderly man at that, weeping is far, far worse.

'I'll come at once,' I assured him while Holmes added for my benefit, 'Mr Neave came here by car, Watson. Is he fit to drive back or shall we take him?'

'We'll see,' I replied. 'Let me get my medical bag first.'

As I hurried up the stairs to collect it from my bedroom, I heard the man, Bill Neave, address Holmes, his voice still husky but a little less tremulous.

'No, sir. I'd rather drive back myself. The car might be needed.'

It was a sensible response and showed to my relief that the man was recovering a little from his earlier breakdown.

'How did you find out there was a doctor here?' Holmes was asking.

'I went to the Fisherman's Arms,' Neave continued. 'I didn't dare drive into Lewes – it's too far – and I thought the landlord at the pub might know of a local doctor or have a phone I could use.'

The conversation continued as I found my bag and the car keys. Holmes was asking, 'Where do you live, Mr Neave?'

It was said in an offhand manner, as if Holmes was merely filling in time while I collected up my equipment.

'Fulworth Hall,' I heard Neave reply.

I was too concerned with the lack of medication in my bag to take in Neave's reply and it was only after I rejoined Holmes and Neave downstairs and we had left the house to drive in the two separate cars that the full significance of Bill Neave's reply struck home.

'Fulworth Hall!' I repeated.

I suddenly realised where I had seen the man before. He had opened the door at Fulworth Hall when Holmes and I had called there in disguise but he had stood so far back that I had only glimpsed his features.

Holmes, who had remained silent until that moment, more concerned with watching through the windscreen for Neave's car to reverse safely from the gateway and turn into the road, looked across at me.

'Yes, Fulworth Hall, Watson. But that was all. The patient's name was not mentioned so we are not quite there yet. We must wait a little longer for that final piece to fall into place and then I think we can safely say the puzzle is solved. And I don't think we shall discover that Neave's wife, if he has one, is the piece we are looking for.'

As we drove up to Fulworth Hall it became clear that Neave had left in a hurry. The gate to the driveway was set wide open, as was the front door. A light was burning, too, in the hall. But Neave allowed us little time to observe these details. He was out of his car in a flash and up the steps to the door, in his haste leaving the lights of his car on as well. I stopped briefly to lean over the driver's seat to switch them off before following the others inside the house.

As he ran, Neave kept calling out a woman's name, 'Mary! Mary!' in a hoarse, urgent voice that continued as he reached the entrance hall, and it crossed my mind, despite the scrambling impetuousness of our arrival, that Neave would hardly address his employer, the Lady in Black, I assumed, in such a manner.

There was an oil lamp burning on a table that was standing at the foot of the stairs, the only illumination to our surroundings, which Neave picked up as he began to mount the steps, and by its uncertain light I looked about me as I followed. It cast long, trembling shadows on the wall, giving me only a vague impression of shabby wallpaper on which lighter squares and oblongs indicated where once paintings must have hung.

As we reached the upper landing, the door facing us opened and the figure of a woman appeared, holding up another lamp. She was dressed in black and for a confused moment I thought she must be *our* Lady in Black until I noticed she was wearing a white apron, suggesting she was not the owner of the house but a servant.

She was a tiny woman, her head barely reaching to

Neave's shoulder, but despite her lack of inches there was a positive, almost authoritative, air about her. She reminded me of a mouse I had once seen peering out from a hole in a skirting board, unaware of my presence: shrewd, bright-eyed, and quick-witted.

'Which of you two is the doctor?' she asked in a low voice.

'I am,' I replied, adding, as I felt Holmes stiffen beside me, 'and this is Mr Holmes, my colleague.'

It was not entirely untrue, I told myself. Holmes had indeed been my colleague for many years and I owed him some return for his loyalty and friendship especially under the present circumstances. He had earned the right to be present when the identity of the Lady in Black was finally solved. Besides, he might be useful in helping to lift the patient if need be or to carry any necessities such as bowls of hot water up and down the stairs.

The woman, Mrs Neave, I assumed, accepted his presence with a nod of her head and he fell in beside me as she opened the door through which she had appeared standing aside to let us enter the room that lay beyond.

It was large, probably the main bedchamber in the house, and, although lit by two lamps, was nevertheless full of shadows, so I could only make out a few features of the room. Like the hall, it had suffered from the spoils of time, the carpet shabby, the curtains faded, the pattern of the wallpaper discoloured and dim.

But it was the bed and the figure lying in it that captured my attention. It was an old-fashioned half-tester with draperies hanging on either side of the headboard so that they framed the woman lying on it, propped up on pillows, leaving just her face and shoulder visible, as if in a portrait, and two frail hands that rested side by side on the quilt. The rest of her body was hidden under a black shawl or robe.

I realised at once that there was nothing I could do for her. Not all the pills or potions in the world could have saved her. She was in the throes of death. The signs were obvious. In my medical career, I had witnessed them many times: the faint, hardly audible breath, the sealed eyelids, the flaccid muscles.

I lifted one of her hands and took it into mine where it lay like a dead leaf on my palm as I reached for her pulse. But I could feel nothing more than a tremor under the skin, like a flutter of a butterfly's wing, and that was all and I gently lowered her hand so that it rested with the other on the coverlet.

She must have been a strikingly attractive woman when young. The features were strongly moulded, in particular the brow and the chin which looked as if they were finely sculptured. The mouth also had the same gentle curve to it. But, like the house, their beauty had faded over time, leaving behind a mere shadow of what it had once been, her dark hair now flecked with grey, the lips no longer relaxing into a smile, the brightness of her eyes quenched.

My action in feeling for her pulse had been noticed by the Neaves who were standing together in the doorway, Bill Neave's arm around his wife's shoulders as if protecting her and, as I replaced the woman's hand, something in my gesture must have warned them that she was dying. They both came towards me, hand in hand now to join me at the bedside where Neave stood as if at attention while his wife fell to her knees, crying out, 'Oh, Miss Eleanor!' in a voice thick with tears.

Holmes, who had remained silent a few paces on the far side, glanced across at me and gave a small nod of his head, a simple enough gesture but one which was complex in its unspoken intimations for it acknowledged the woman's imminent death, his own sadness at her passing and also his recognition of the significance of her name. The last piece of the puzzle had been found, it said, and the mystery of the Lady in Black's identity finally solved.

She died shortly afterwards, the last flicker of life extinguished. I felt it expire under my fingers as the faint tremor of her pulse ceased.

For a few moments, I could do nothing except stand there, holding her wrist between my fingers and gazing down at her as it dawned on me for the first time that I was looking into the face of Eleanor Sutton, Hetty and George Sutton's daughter, granddaughter of Henry Trevalyan and that other Eleanor, the one she had been named for: Eleanor Lockhart of Abbot's farm.

And the Lady in Black.

Mary Neave was asking, 'She's dead, isn't she, doctor?' to which there was no reply except, 'I am afraid so.'

'Then,' Mrs Neave continued, rising to her feet, her tears staunched and her lips firm, 'we must lay her out properly. That's the last thing I can do for my poor darling.'

It was Holmes who stepped in at this point.

'Wait!' he told her. 'You can't manage it on your own. You must have help.' Turning to her husband, he continued, 'Come downstairs with me, Mr Neave. We must arrange for someone to come and assist her.'

I was relieved by Holmes' positiveness in taking charge of the situation and followed meekly as, a lamp in hand, he led the way out of the room and down the stairs, Bill Neave falling into step behind us.

At Holmes' instigation, we entered a room on the left of the hall that I assumed after a brief inspection was probably the breakfast room in those far-off days when the house was inhabited and living people had occupied the place. Discarded and empty apart from a few chairs and a table, it had the same melancholy air of the rest of the house we had already entered, abandoned and forlorn.

But Holmes was not in the least discouraged by the setting. Pulling forward three of the chairs to form a semicircle, he sat down, indicating to Neave and myself to do the same. As I did so, I noticed we were facing a pair of French windows that overlooked the cove and, as I took my place, I could see through the dusty glass in the faint light of the moon not only the beach and the wooden steps that led down to it but that stone armchair where the Lady in Black had once sat, looking out to sea.

If Holmes was aware of the poignancy of the view, he made no sign of it.

'Now,' he said, addressing both Neave and myself, 'we must arrange matters so that not too much is expected of Mrs Neave. I suggest therefore that we appoint another woman to help her.'

'Mrs B?' I interposed as his gaze fell on me and Neave seemed too distressed to offer any advice. Although I was not at all sure that she was the right choice, I could think of no other woman in our limited female circle.

Holmes' reaction was immediate.

'Great heavens no, Watson! She is the last person to ask. I was thinking of the landlady at the Fisherman's Arms. She is a sensible, cheerful woman. And I further suggest that I ask her myself. She knows me and I can better explain the situation to her.'

'I'll drive you there,' I offered, half-rising to my feet.

'No, Watson. It's only a five-minute walk. Stay here. You may be needed.'

As he said it, he glanced towards Neave who was sitting like a man who has only just regained consciousness, his head hanging low and his elbows resting on his knees, and I gave a small nod of agreement.

'I shan't be long.' Holmes promised and, on this occasion, he meant it, returning in less than a quarter of an hour accompanied by Mrs Berry, a capable woman whom I had seen in the Fisherman's Arms, serving behind the bar. I noticed she was carrying bed linen and towels folded over her arm.

At her arrival, Neave immediately brightened up, lifting his head and showing signs of eagerness to go upstairs with her to join his wife. This time it was I who dissuaded him from leaving the room. I knew from my own experience that what was happening up there was a ritual, like birth, that was exclusively for women only.

To my relief, Neave made no protest but remained seated, his eyes swivelling from Holmes to myself as if seeking solace or an answer to an unanswerable question.

It was Holmes who spoke first in the voice of an old family friend.

'I am so sorry, Mr Neave,' he said. 'Had you known her for long?'

It was only a small, gentle prompt but it opened up Neave's heart as if it had unlocked a whole reservoir of dammed-up memories and emotions which came gushing out in a flood.

'Oh, Mr Holmes!' he cried. 'What's me and Mary going to do? She meant the world to us! Such a lovely child! And now she's left us!'

'When did you first meet her?' Holmes asked.

'Oh years ago, sir! It was when her mother was married to Mr Sutton who was still alive at the time. They had the baby, Eleanor, by then and Mrs Sutton took us on as extra help, me in the garden and seeing to the car – they'd not long got rid of the horses and the carriages and I could drive, you see – and my wife to help the nanny with the baby. Me and Mary was very young at the time – we hadn't been married all that long – so we were over the moon when Mrs Sutton took us on. Her husband was well known. Men would take their caps off when they passed him in the street. So it was a great honour to work for him and his wife.

'Then bit by bit, we went up in the world. The nanny retired and Mary became the nursemaid and me the chauffeur. Their little girl was only a toddler at the time.'

'So you knew her quite well?' Holmes asked. 'What was she like?'

'Little Eleanor? Oh, a beautiful child. As pretty as a picture. A right little sweetheart.'

'And her mother, Mrs Sutton?'

'Once she got over the shock of her husband's death, she was a lovely lady. Although after he died, she was never quite the same again. Very sad. And the little girl as well. But all the same, we couldn't have asked for a better person to work for.'

'Did you ever meet any of Mrs Sutton's family?' Holmes continued.

'Mr and Mrs Trevalyan you mean, sir? Yes, we did after Mr Trevalyan's death that is. I think there'd been some trouble between him and his daughter in the past and they'd never met since. Not much was said about him but, reading between the lines so to say, I got the impression he was a very difficult man, liked to have his own way. Anyway, after he died, we used to drive down to their house in Fulworth, me and Mary and little Eleanor so that she could meet her grandmother. Her name was Eleanor as well. I think Miss Eleanor was named after her.'

'What about the visits to Fulworth? Did she play on the beach?' Holmes asked in an easy tone, not giving any special emphasis to the question and Neave seemed to accept it as part of the ongoing conversation.

'Oh, the beach!' he exclaimed. 'She loved the beach. Mrs Trevalyan had the steps specially built so we could get down to the beach from the garden. Mrs Trevalyan would come as well until she got too old to manage the climb. And I took her several times to visit other relations she had living in a big farmhouse down in Barton. Little Eleanor used to feed the chickens and have a go on the swing they had in the orchard. She loved that, too!'

So another piece of the puzzle had dropped into place, I thought, with the reference to the cove at Fulworth even though Holmes had laid no special emphasis on it.

He was saying in the same easy, relaxed manner, 'It sounds as if she had a wonderful childhood.'

'Oh, she did, sir. She certainly did,' Neave agreed. 'And we loved it, too. You see me and Mary had no children so she was like a daughter to us.'

'And then?' Holmes asked.

Neave hesitated and I wondered if we had lost him. He would clam up and that would be that. But, undaunted, Holmes cocked his head, inviting further enlightenment.

'What about Roger Sinclair?' he asked, in the same easy tone of voice.

Neave's uncertainty lasted for several long moments in which he locked his hands together and stared down at his feet. I was sure Holmes had gone too far and Neave would confide in us no further, leaving gaps in the Lady in Black story.

In the long silence, Holmes and I gazed down on the top of Neave's head, willing him to speak; at least, I was willing him and so too, I imagined, was Holmes for he sat perfectly motionless, his eyes on Neave while the atmosphere grew thicker by the second. But it could not be maintained; it had to break and it was Neave who finally broke it.

Without lifting his head, he spoke at last, his voice flat and exhausted as if the spirit had been knocked out of him.

'He was a wicked man, Mr Holmes. Wicked. There's no other word for it. It's him to blame for everything that's happened to Miss Eleanor and her mother.'

'How did they meet?' Holmes asked, gently.

Neave raised his face towards Holmes, his expression haggard, and, when he spoke, it was in short broken sentences.

'He was someone from London, one of Mrs Sutton's friends who brought him along one evening. After that he kept turning up. Then Mr Sutton died but he still kept coming, brought flowers, sat with her to cheer Miss Eleanor up, or so he said. Me and Mary didn't take to him from the start – he was worming his way in, we thought – turning on the charm; not that Mrs Sutton could see it.'

His voice broke at this point and the tears that had gathered in his eyes began to spill over his cheeks.

'Sorry, sir. Sorry,' he muttered, wiping them away on the sleeve of his coat. 'It upsets me when I think of it.'

I saw his face begin to crumple up as if he had lost control of the muscles, a symptom I had seen in the features of two of my patients before they suffered a complete breakdown and I realised we must stop questioning him. So, glancing across at Holmes, I shook my head briefly, before leaning forward to touch the man's hand.

'It's all right, Mr Neave,' I assured him. 'There's no need to explain. We know what happened.'

To my astonishment, Neave seized my hand, grasping it as a drowning man might clutch at a broken branch or a handful of grass.

'He took everything she owned!' he cried out. 'Everything! And left her with nothing! Oh, the poor woman! By that time, her mother had died as well. "I have no one!" she kept crying out. "No one!" It broke her heart. I hope to God he rots in hell!'

'I hope so too,' I interjected.

Holmes, however, managed to preserve his impassive attitude to the situation, untouched, it seemed, by any emotional response – that insensitivity of his that in the past I had regarded as cold-blooded and unfeeling. This reaction on my part also disturbed me deeply for I thought I had come to terms with this side of Holmes' nature and had accepted it without question.

But it seemed, thank God, that I had misjudged him for, leaning forward, he took Bill Neave's other hand in his and so we sat, hand in hand, each of us in our own way mourning the tragedy that had overwhelmed its participants.

CHAPTER FOURTEEN

The silence was broken ten minutes later by the arrival of Mary Neave, carrying a lamp, who tapped on the door before entering to announce, 'Mrs Berry and me have finished upstairs, Dr Watson. I don't know if you want to see her for yourselves? If you do, everything's ready.'

'Thank you. I'd like to,' I said adding, 'what about Mrs Berry? Should one of us take her home?'

'She's already left, sir. She'll be all right. Her husband Reg is waiting up for her. So if you'd like to follow me. You, too, Mr Holmes if you wish.'

I turned to Bill Neave, who still sat, head bowed.

'Will you come as well?' I asked him, thinking he would be better off in bed, with a glass of brandy.

To my relief, he shook his head.

'He'll be all right,' Mary Neave assured us. 'I'll see to him later.'

So Holmes and I left him there and followed the diminutive figure of Mary Neave out of the room in silence, broken only when we reached the upper landing at the head of the stairs. It was here Mary Neave halted outside the door that led into the bedroom where the Lady in Black was lying, and turned to face us.

Because of her height it was the first time I had studied her features in any detail, considering her to be of less significance than her husband, and what I saw, surprised me. Despite her lack of inches, she carried herself proudly and her expression was direct and confident.

'You must excuse my husband,' she told us. 'He's taken the whole business very badly. But he'll be all right. I'll see to him later. In the meantime, if you care to come with me . . .'

Opening the bedroom door, she stood aside to let us enter.

What we saw as we passed her and stepped inside was astonishing. The room had been transformed, the solitary oil lamp replaced by an array of silver candlesticks, at least half a dozen of them, displayed along the dressing table, the mirror reflecting each of their individual flames and doubling them so that they lit up the room with a radiance that seemed unearthly. More candles burnt on either side of the bed, drawing our attention to the bed itself and the figure that lay on it.

It was our Lady in Black, but transformed as if by some enchanted metamorphosis. Dressed in white this time, in a high-necked, old-fashioned nightdress with lace at the neck and wrists, her hair brushed out and lying in loose braids against the pillows, her features were now completely relaxed, all creases smoothed away; she was at last at rest.

There were four chairs drawn up by the bed, two on each side: their positioning a deliberate arrangement, making it clear that this was no informal gathering. The women had decided it was to be a wake.

Holmes shot a glance at me, surprised but not derisive in any way, simply accepting the situation as he sat down. I took the chair opposite his so that we were facing one another, while Mary Neave seated herself beside me.

I had sat next to the dead before, including my first wife, but had never attended so formal a gathering before and I looked across at Mary Neave, wondering what we were supposed to do. Pray? Give a eulogy? Remain silent?

It was Holmes who spoke up.

'I am so sorry, Mrs Neave,' he began.

'Oh, don't be,' she replied in a perfectly natural

tone of voice, brisk and to the point, no sign of tears or distress. 'She's better off where she is, poor love. We'll miss her though, Bill and me. She was a wonderful lady who deserved better.'

I realised that nothing more was expected of us, thank God, than a normal conversation.

'She had a hard time, I understand,' I remarked.

'Indeed she did,' Mary Neave replied. 'And she deserved none of it.'

Holmes shifted about restlessly in his chair and I knew from the expression on his face that he could not maintain this exchange of commiserations about the dead woman however heartfelt they might be. He wanted something stronger than that, more positive and factual.

Throwing back his head, as if to break some unseen thread that bound us all together, he said in a clear, hard voice, 'What about the silverware Mrs Neave? Why was that taken?'

I found his response disturbing under the circumstances. Could he not show more sympathy and understanding than this? I had not experienced that cold, almost callous side to his nature since our old days in Baker Street. But before I could protest, Mary Neave herself had spoken up.

Looking directly across the bed at him, she said, 'You mean the stuff we stole from Melchett Manor?'

'Yes, I do,' Holmes replied, having the grace to

look, at least, taken aback by her directness.

She nodded towards the candlesticks arranged on the dressing table and beside the bed.

'They were hers, Mr Holmes. Her grandmother, Mrs Trevalyan, left her all the family silver. There were other things as well: pictures, pieces of jewellery, things Miss Eleanor knew from her childhood. Then *he* started taking them and selling them off.'

'Roger Sinclair, you mean?' Holmes asked.

'Oh, so you've heard of him, have you?' she asked, bright-eyed. 'You know what Bill and me used to call him? The scavenger. He'd snap up anything valuable you left lying about and sell it; even the house Mr Sutton had built for her. We were living then in a little old cottage in the rough part of town. But he'd still turn up even there. He knew she still had some money and investments Mrs Trevalyan had left her in trust. And then I caught him one day trying to force himself on her. Don't tell Bill that. It'll only upset him even more. That's when I made up my mind.'

'To do what?' Holmes asked.

'To clear out, of course,' Mary Neave said, as if any fool should have known the answer. 'I said to Bill, "I'm not putting up with it any longer. We'll go and take Miss Eleanor with us." I'd gone through the papers Mrs Sutton's solicitor had drawn up – Miss Eleanor was in no state to deal with anything like that – and found out she had £100 in cash as well as stocks and shares so I got Miss Eleanor to sign up for the lot to be withdrawn before *he* got his hands on it. "Right! Start packing!" I said to Bill when the bank statement came through. "We're leaving!" "Where to?" he asked. "Fulworth", I said. "We're taking her home." It was what she wanted. She kept crying all the time, "I want to go home! I want to go home!" Like a little child who's lost.'

'And then?' Holmes asked obviously fascinated by her story.

'Once the money was safe in her account, we bought a van, packed everything in it and drove off to Sussex.'

'Did you know that Fulworth Hall was empty and up for renting?' I asked, like Holmes bemused by Mary Neave's narration.

Mary Neave gave me a smile.

'No, we didn't,' she replied. 'We hoped there'd be somewhere cheap in the village that we could buy or lease for the three of us.'

She broke off here to put an unexpected question to Holmes and myself.

'Do you believe in fate?' she asked.

Holmes and I looked at each other, not sure how to respond. There was no need to anyway for she answered it for herself.

'I do,' she said. 'I never had before but I did then. We were driving down the hill towards the village when we saw the 'To Let' sign by the gate of Fulworth Hall. It was a godsend; sent by God; and it was meant to happen. I'm sure of that. So we went straight back to Lewes to the estate agent and arranged to pay the rent for it there and then.

'The man warned us it was in a poor state. It had been empty for several years. But we didn't care. Me and Bill cleaned it up as best as we could and we bought one or two bits of furniture to go in it from a second-hand shop, such as the bed,' nodding at it, before breaking off to address Holmes.

'Is that all, sir?'

He responded immediately.

'No, Mrs Neave. It's far from all. There's a lot left that still hasn't been explained.'

She accepted the rebuke without protest. Straightening herself up, she looked him directly in the face.

'You mean us breaking into Melchett Manor and stealing some of the silver?'

'I do indeed. Tell me what happened.'

She was not easily cowed.

'There's not a lot to say, sir,' she replied in a matter-of-fact tone. 'We knew what Roger Sinclair had stolen from her. I'd kept a list of everything he'd taken down to the last teaspoon. It was not long after we'd moved to Fulworth when Bill had gone into Lewes to do some shopping – we steered clear of Fulworth village in case there was any gossip about us. Anyway, he bought a copy of the local newspaper, the *Lewes Gazette*, and there was an item in it about the owners of Melchett Manor buying a new selection of silverware at an auction to add to their collection and they'd decided to put it all on display. Several pieces were described. One of them was a little casket with silver roses on the lid. It was one of Miss Eleanor's best-loved pieces her grandmother had left her. She kept asking where some of the things had gone, "Where's my christening cup?" She'd say. Or "Have you seen the silver bowl we used to put flowers in?" It distressed her. I hated to see her cry.'

'So you decided to take them back?' Holmes asked.

'I'm afraid we did, sir. Bill went to look around the place on one of the open days and thought we could get in without too much trouble.'

'Through the pantry window?'

'Yes, sir. I did that. I was the smallest. Bill was too big and we couldn't expect Miss Eleanor to do it.'

It was said in the same calm almost dismissive manner.

'You took her with you?' I asked, taken aback.

'Of course,' she said. 'She couldn't be left alone. She was too ill by then.'

'Ill?' I repeated.

'In the head, sir. She'd lost her mind. There was no knowing what she might do.'

'Like going down to the beach in the middle of the night and sitting on one of the rocks?' Holmes put in.

She gave him a quick glance.

'You saw her, sir?'

'A couple of times. I noticed your husband on the last occasion leading her back to the house.'

'Oh, I see,' was the only reply she granted him before adding, 'is that everything?'

'Almost,' he replied. 'There's still the matter of the crypt to be dealt with. You kept some of the silver down there. Why?'

'Because Bill thought he'd seen Roger Sinclair one day in Lewes so we decided to lock all the silver up somewhere safe. But I think Bill was mistaken. It wasn't Sinclair he'd seen.'

'How did you get into the crypt?' Holmes continued.

'With a key,' she replied with a small wry smile as much as to say 'Isn't that obvious?' But as Holmes made no response, she added, 'The old grandfather, Henry Trevalyan, left one for everybody in the family so that they could be buried with him, I suppose, and he'd still be Lord of the Manor even after he died. The solicitor gave it to us when he sorted out Miss Eleanor's papers.' After a little pause in which she regarded us both with that same amused expression, she went on, 'And if you've ever wondered why she always wore black it was because of the death of her mother and grandmother in the same year. It was then that her mind began to go wrong. There was too much grief for her to bear any longer.'

'Yes, I understand,' Holmes said while I simply bent my head in agreement.

But Mrs Neave had not quite finished with us.

'Now let me ask both of you something. What's going to happen to Bill and me? I suppose the police will have to be told about us stealing the silver from Melchett Manor and we'll have to go to prison? I'm right, aren't I?'

Holmes and I exchanged glances and it was he who answered.

'Leave it with me, Mrs Neave. We'll discuss this after the funeral.'

And with that, he rose from his chair and walked towards the door, leaving me with no option but to follow him.

'Discuss?' I demanded when we set off in the car to return to Holmes' cottage. 'What good can we do in discussing it? They'll be charged with theft and go to prison. There's the end of it.'

'Oh, Watson, my dear fellow, you must learn to be a little less pessimistic. There are ways and means. Trust me.'

I do not know what 'ways and means' Holmes used. I only know that he spent a long time on the telephone speaking to Inspector Bardle the following day and that by the time the funeral was arranged something, somehow had been agreed and all was well. He had also, I found out later, arranged with the solicitor for the Neaves to inherit Eleanor Sutton's settlement of the stocks and shares.

'You see,' Holmes remarked, 'fate does sometimes turn up trumps, like Mrs Neave's godsend. But don't ask how it happened, Watson.'

I stayed on for a few more days to attend Eleanor Sutton's funeral. I felt I had to be there and my wife agreed.

It was a moving ceremony. St Botolph's was packed with people from the village who had known and remembered her mother and grandmother, and Eleanor herself as a child. Mrs B, who was among the congregation, said there was more there than had been for Henry Trevalyan's funeral. And rightly too.

After the service, the coffin was driven away to Barton for a private internment with just the family attending and she was buried with her mother, as I'm sure she herself would have wanted, under the white cross, her name and dates added to the marble book that lay open on the grave.

Fate also intervened, I felt sure, a littler later when

Langdale Pike telephoned Holmes to inform him of Roger Sinclair's own fate. He had died, Pike said, of cirrhosis of the liver, alone in some shabby little hotel room in London, and had been buried in a pauper's grave.

'And, as Mrs B might have said,' Holmes continued, 'serves him right!'

I must confess that I agreed with him completely.

ALSO BY JUNE THOMSON

The Secret Files of Sherlock Holmes

An investigation into the disappearance of a headwaiter, his locked wardrobe and a baker's van is the first case in this compelling cache of reports. In Dr Watson's compendium of secret files the fantastic Sherlock Holmes embarks on a bird-watching 'holiday' in Cornwall leading to the unmasking of a spy; two glasses of port conduce the apprehension of an artful burglar; and a young woman is found dead in the Thames.

The Secret Documents of Sherlock Holmes

Secret documents belonging to Dr John Watson have remained undisclosed in a safe at his bank in Charing Cross for years until now. These are cases of trickery and the uncanny: from the mysterious disappearance of Sir Ainsworth's daughter, along with her horse and groom, to the theft of the Pope's treasured cameos from outside the British Museum, to the repulsive story of the red leech and the terrible death of a banker – can Sherlock Holmes and his trusty side-kick Dr Watson unravel them all?

The Secret Chronicles of Sherlock Holmes

Never-before-seen cases meticulously chronicled by Dr Watson are published for the first time. Crimes of intrigue and suspense: Marguerite Rossignol, the French Nightingale, is found backstage of the Cambridge music hall strangled with one of her own stockings; the British Prime Minister is sent a dead rat and a threatening letter; and a girl drugged on morphine is somehow linked to a Californian goldmine.

The Secret Journals of Sherlock Holmes

As Dr Watson's secret manuscripts are revealed to the public, a multitude of previously unseen cases come to light. An American millionaire receives threatening letters from a sinister Black Hand . . . A mysterious box terrifies a shopkeeper . . . Holmes and Watson feel the influence of an old enemy from beyond the grave . . . And a tragedy occurs which Sherlock Holmes will never be able to forgive himself for failing to prevent.